HELP!
I'M TRAPPED IN THE
FIRST DAY OF SCHOOL

Other Books by Todd Strasser

Beyond the Reef

The Complete Computer Personality Program

The Diving Bell

Free Willy (novelization)

Friends Till the End

Help! I'm Trapped in My Teacher's Body

Home Alone™ (novelization)

Home Alone 2™ (novelization)

The Mall from Outer Space

HELP!
I'M TRAPPED IN THE
FIRST DAY OF SCHOOL

Todd Strasser

AN
APPLE
PAPERBACK

SCHOLASTIC INC.
New York Toronto London Auckland Sydney

No part of this publication may be reproduced in whole or in part, or stored in a retrieval system, or transmitted in any form or by any means, electronic, mechanical, photocopying, recording, or otherwise, without written permission of the publisher. For information regarding permission, write to Scholastic Inc., 555 Broadway, New York, NY 10012

ISBN 0-590-48647-0

Copyright © 1994 by Todd Strasser.
All rights reserved. Published by Scholastic Inc.
APPLE PAPERBACKS is a registered trademark of Scholastic Inc.

12   9/9

Printed in the U.S.A.   40

First Scholastic printing, September 1994

To Leigh and Terry

HELP!
I'M TRAPPED IN THE
FIRST DAY OF SCHOOL

1

DAY ONE

Beep . . . beep . . . beep! The alarm on the night table went off and I opened my eyes. I'd just had the weirdest dream about a groundhog named Bill. Why would I dream about a groundhog? I didn't have time to wonder about it. Today was the first day of school. As much as I hated going back, there was one thing I was looking forward to. This year Alex Silver and I were going to rule.

"Ready to conquer the world, Mr. Big Shot?" my sister Jessica asked when I came into the kitchen. She was sitting at the kitchen table, having a bowl of granola.

"Drop dead." I pulled out a new box of chocolate Pop-Tarts from the cupboard and tore it open.

Over the summer Jessica had changed from

being your average pain-in-the-butt big sister to being a super pain-in-the-butt PC big sister. PC stood for Politically Correct, which basically meant she had become a vegetarian, was into a million dumb causes, and always took the side of the underdog. She couldn't go anywhere without six different red, or maroon, or green ribbons pinned to her clothes, which were all black.

Today she was wearing a tight black leotard and a short black skirt. She'd also dyed her hair black and had her nose pierced with a small gold hoop.

To me, PC stood for Pea-brained Cretin.

"You're being really immature, you know," she said.

"Look who's talking," I replied as I put two Pop-Tarts in the toaster. "Just because you're going into tenth grade doesn't mean you're Miss Know-It-All."

"I know that Alex Silver is really bad news," Jessica said. "Ever since you got to know him, you've changed."

"I've changed?" I had to laugh. "Look at you. Every day you dress like you're going to a funeral. And what's the story with that nose ring? I mean, doesn't it get all crusty on the inside?"

"See?" Jessica said. "That's not Jake Sherman talking. That's Alex Silver. You started hanging around with him this summer and now you think being gross, mean, and disgusting makes you cool."

"Get lost." I really couldn't stand her moralizing.

"Whatever happened to Andy Kent and Josh Hopka?" Jessica asked.

"They're still around," I said. My Pop-Tarts popped out of the toaster.

"You never see them anymore."

"Because they're dorks, okay?"

"They used to be your best friends."

"Yeah, well, that was then and this is now." I picked up my Pop-Tarts and stood at the kitchen counter next to the window. Mom and Dad had already left for work.

"Look, Jake, I know the eighth-graders picked on you on your first day of sixth grade," Jessica said. "But that doesn't mean you have to pick on sixth-graders now that *you're* in eighth grade."

"Who said I was going to pick on anybody?" I asked defensively.

Jessica gave me a knowing look. "I heard you talking on the phone last night to Alex about calling yourselves the Knights of Wedgy and getting all the sixth-graders."

I turned and looked out the kitchen window so that Jessica wouldn't see the smile on my face. It was true. Alex and I planned to start the year by wedgying everyone in sight.

From our window I could see the bus stop at the corner of Magnolia Street and Bay Drive. A small kid with short blond hair and glasses was standing on the corner, looking around nervously as if he was worried he wasn't in the right place.

"Do you believe it?" I said. "The bus won't even be here for fifteen minutes and some kid's already waiting. He *has* to be a sixth-grader."

"I remember *you* got to the bus stop early on your first day of middle school, too," Jessica said as she cleared her bowl from the table.

"Did not," I said.

"Did too." Jessica put her dish in the sink and squinted out the window. "I've never seen him before. Must be new."

First victim, I thought, smiling to myself. Out of the corner of my eye, I noticed that Jessica was staring at me.

"Jake . . ." she said in a warning tone.

"What?" I asked innocently.

"I know what you're thinking. You really ought to grow up."

"You mean, wear a ring in my nose and dress like an undertaker?" I asked.

Jessica gritted her teeth and made a fist. I could tell I'd made her really mad.

Suddenly in the background, the town's fire siren went off — *Whaaaaa-O-Whaaaaa-O-Whaaaa!* — alerting the volunteer firemen of a fire.

4

A moment later it was followed by the sound of a car honking in our driveway.

"That's Cathy," Jessica said. "Her sister's giving us a ride to school. Want to come?"

"No way," I said. "I'm meeting Alex at the bus stop."

"Of course." My sister sneered. "You're Sir Jake, a Knight of Wedgy now. It's time to start your little reign of terror."

2

Outside it was still summery. The trees were green and insects buzzed around in the warm air. As I walked down to the bus stop, I couldn't help feeling good. Today me and Alex were finally on the top of the heap.

Eeeeiiiiirrrrnnnn! Eeeeiiiiirrrrnnnn! A big red-and-silver pumper truck raced down Bay Drive with its lights flashing. A couple of seconds later another fire truck shot past. It looked like they were heading a few blocks away. I didn't think much of it. Most of the time it just turned out to be a false alarm.

By now Alex had arrived at the bus stop, along with half a dozen other kids. Alex was sporting a new buzz cut and a diamond stud earring. He was wearing a black T-shirt, jeans, and cool boots.

When he saw me, he raised his hand. "Sir Jake, dude!"

"Sir Alex, bud!" We gave each other high fives and glanced around at the other kids, who looked back at us nervously. For the first time in our lives, we were the biggest kids at the bus stop.

"Are we the Knights of Wedgy?" Alex asked loudly enough for everyone to hear.

"Yes!" I said.

"Are we bad?" Alex asked with a grin.

"Yes!"

"Do we wedgy?"

"Most righteously, yes!"

Slap! We gave each other another high five. Then Alex turned to the little group around us. "Everyone will now stand shoulder-to-shoulder at attention," he ordered.

"What if we don't?" asked Robbie Bayuk, a seventh-grade wise guy.

"You'll be wedgied by royal order of the king," Alex threatened.

Robbie quickly got into line with the others. The only one who didn't get into line was the new blond kid with the glasses. He was wearing a blue short-sleeve shirt and neatly pressed khaki slacks and was carrying a new light-green backpack.

Alex peered down at him and rubbed his chin. "Sir Jake," he called to me. "What manner of creature is this?"

"Why, I believe it's a dweeb, Sir Alex," I replied.

Alex nodded. "Tell me, dweeb, have you trouble hearing?"

The kid shook his head.

"Then why aren't you standing with the others?"

"Uh, well, I was just wondering what a wedgy was?"

The kids in line all snickered. Alex stepped closer, and the kid stepped back, frightened.

"Do my ears deceive me?" Alex asked. "Truly have you no idea what a wedgy is?"

The kid shook his head.

Alex looked over at me. "Tell me, Sir Jake, what thinketh you of this?"

"I thinketh we must learn this dweeb's name," I replied. "And from what strange wedgiless land he has come."

"What is your name, dweeb?" Alex asked.

"Uh, Oliver," the kid stammered. "But everyone calls me Ollie."

"Ollie?" Alex repeated in disbelief.

"Be that a dorkish name or what?" I asked.

"It's . . . it's not like I had a choice," Ollie replied in a quavering voice.

"And from what strange wedgiless land do you come, Dweeb Ollie?" Alex asked.

"Uh, Ohio," Ollie said. "Near Cleveland."

"And have they no wedgies near Cleveland, Dweeb Ollie of Ohio?" I asked.

"Not where I come from," Ollie said.

"Tell us, Dweeb Ollie of Ohio," said Alex. "Who picks out your clothes for you?"

"Uh, my mom."

"Is this not cute?" I grinned. "His mommy still dresses him in the morning."

"And you really don't know what a wedgy is?" Alex asked.

Ollie shook his head. Alex and I exchanged a serious look.

"You know what this means, Sir Jake?" Alex said.

"Death?" I guessed.

"Next time," Alex said. "But for now, he must run around the block."

"Now?" Ollie's jaw dropped.

"Forsooth." Alex nodded.

"But I'll miss the bus," Ollie said.

"Not if you hurry."

"But . . ." Ollie whimpered.

Alex bent down and hooked his fingers through the bottom laces of Ollie's brand-new white tennis shoes. Then he pulled hard, tightening the laces all the way up.

"Ow!" Ollie cried and stepped back.

"Dost thou know what that was, Dweeb Ollie of Ohio?" Alex asked, straightening up.

Ollie shook his head.

"A mere shoe wedgy," Alex informed him. "And nothing compared to what will happen next if you do not get your butt in motion."

Ollie started to back away.

9

"Now!" Alex shouted.

Ollie took off down the sidewalk. I figured he'd get back in time to catch the bus.

"Like a true dweeb." Alex crossed his arms and turned to me. "Hast thou any gum, Sir Jake?"

"Why, yes, Sir Alex." I pulled a pack of Juicy Fruit out of my T-shirt pocket and gave him a stick. Meanwhile, across the street, Mr. Mac-Dowell came out of his house. He was an old guy with thin white hair. We watched him walk stiffly to his garage.

"Observe this," Alex said, going across the street. While the old man went into his garage and got into his car, Alex moved one of Mr. MacDowell's garbage cans into his driveway. Then he came back across the street.

A few seconds later Mr. MacDowell backed his car down the driveway.

Crunck! As the car reached the curb, it hit the garbage can, knocking it over and spilling out white garbage bags.

Muttering to himself, Mr. MacDowell slowly got out of his car.

"Clap," Alex ordered the sixth- and seventh-graders.

No one clapped.

"I said *clap!*" Alex snarled.

The kids started clapping. Across the street Mr. MacDowell winced as he bent down and put the garbage bags back in the can. Then he straightened up and pointed a bony finger at us.

"It's not funny!" he said angrily. "You kids ought to show some respect."

Just then the school bus turned the corner and stopped.

"What about the new kid?" Robbie Bayuk asked.

We looked down the block. There was no sign of Ollie.

"Me thinks he shall have to learn to run faster," Alex said with a shrug, and climbed on.

I hesitated, sort of hoping Ollie would sprint around the corner. After all, it was the kid's first day. Did he really have to miss the bus?

3

Exercising our eighth-grade privileges, the Knights of Wedgy kicked all the younger kids out of the back of the bus and sat down. At school we found our new lockers.

"Cool, Sir Alex, we are almost next to each other," I said as we stood at our lockers. We both took out the letters we'd gotten over the summer with our new combinations.

Brinnnggg! The homeroom bell rang. Alex and I were just about to go in when we heard rapid footsteps coming down the hall toward us. We turned and saw who it was.

"Why, it's Dweeb Ollie of Ohio," Alex said with a nasty grin. "You have arrived!"

Ollie's face was red and he was breathing so hard that he couldn't talk.

"Is it possible that Dweeb Ollie of Ohio ran all the way to school?" Alex asked.

Ollie nodded and gasped. "I . . . I can't find my homeroom."

"And what room might that be, Ollie boy?" Alex asked, giving me a wink.

"One-oh-six."

Alex gave him an awestruck look. "Forsooth! You must travel all the way to the other side of school. Take the stairs at the end of this hall. When you get up to the second floor, turn right and go all the way to the end of that hall. Then make another right and go to the end of *that* hall. Your destination will be right around there."

"I go up the stairs, then right down the first hall, right down the second and I'm there?" Ollie repeated.

"That is correct," Alex said. "But you must hurry, Dweeb Ollie of Ohio. You must not be late for homeroom on your first day."

Ollie took off and ran all the way down the hall and up the stairs. As soon as he was out of sight, I cracked up. Room 106 was only two doors away!

"He'll never find it now!" Alex cried, giving me a high five. "He'll probably be lost until lunch!"

I had to admit that it was kind of funny. Besides, Ollie wouldn't get into trouble. Everyone expected sixth-graders to get lost on the first day of school. Still laughing, Alex and I went into homeroom.

"Hello, boys," someone said.

We turned and found Ms. Rogers, who'd started as a new teacher when we were in sixth grade.

She had black, wavy hair and big, blue eyes and used to call me her favorite troublemaker.

"Hey, Ms. Rogers, how was your summer?" I asked.

"Wonderful, Jake," she said, showing off a gold wedding band on her ring finger. "Look what I just got."

"You mean . . .?" My jaw dropped.

Ms. Rogers smiled and nodded. "Mr. Dirksen and I finally tied the knot."

"Wow, congratulations," I said, noticing that Alex was giving me a funny look.

"Does that mean now we have to call you Mrs. *Dork*sen?" Alex asked.

The smile disappeared from Ms. Rogers's face. "No, we decided I'd still use my maiden name. Now go find your seats, boys."

We went to the back of the room and sat. The seat next to me was empty. Alex slouched way down in his chair.

"How come you're so friendly to her?" he whispered while Ms. Rogers took attendance.

"I don't know," I whispered back. "Guess I've always thought she was okay."

"A teacher!" Alex wrinkled his nose as if it were impossible for any teacher to be okay.

"Jake Sherman?" Ms. Rogers called.

"Here." I raised my hand.

"Alex Silver?"

Alex gave her a cool little half-wave.

14

"Amber Sweeny?" Ms. Rogers called.

No one answered.

"Ever heard of her?" Alex whispered.

"She must be new," I whispered back.

Ms. Rogers finished taking attendance and picked up a blue sheet of paper. "Principal Blanco has asked all the homeroom teachers to read this bulletin," she said, clearing her throat. " 'Hello, and welcome back to school. We here at the Burt Itchupt Middle School hope that you all had a wonderful summer and that you're ready to buckle down for a really exciting year of school — ' "

"Really exciting?" muttered Alex. A couple of kids around us giggled.

"Ahem." Ms. Rogers cleared her throat again and continued. " 'Every year we welcome a new group of sixth-graders, and this year is no exception. We ask that all seventh- and eighth-graders show our new students the courtesy and respect we are accustomed to here at Burt Itchupt.' "

"Burp It Up," Alex whispered, and the kids chuckled.

Ms. Rogers stopped reading and gave him the evil eye. "That's enough, Alex."

Alex grinned at everyone. I guess he liked the attention. Then he raised his hand. "Uh, Ms. Rogers, I'm not sure I understand what you mean by courtesy and respect."

"Well," Ms. Rogers replied. "In your case, Alex, that would mean don't give them incorrect directions, don't jam their lockers, don't make them sing, or force them into the bathroom used by the opposite sex."

Alex raised his hand again. "What about wedgies?"

"I would imagine that any student caught giving wedgies will be immediately suspended from school."

"Would that include nature wedgies?" Alex asked.

The class tittered.

"What is a nature wedgy?" Ms. Rogers asked.

"It's like a regular wedgy, except you throw in rocks and pinecones and burrs and stuff."

"Ew!" "Gross!" "Give me a break!" All around the classroom kids made disgusted sounds.

"I would think that anyone caught giving a nature wedgy would be subject to the harshest punishment Mr. Blanco could issue," Ms. Rogers replied.

Alex raised his hand again.

"Now what, Alex?" Ms. Rogers asked.

"What about a Melvin?"

More chuckles spread through the room.

Ms. Rogers gave him a blank look.

"It's a wedgy from the front," Alex explained.

"Ugh!" the guys in the room groaned. Just the thought of it was enough to make you ill.

"No Melvins," said Ms. Rogers firmly.

Then the door opened and a girl stepped into

the classroom. She had long straight-brown hair, almond-shaped green eyes, and smooth flawless skin. She bit the corner of her lip nervously.

"*Hubba hubba!*" Alex whispered under his breath.

"Can I help you?" Ms. Rogers asked the girl.

"Is this Ms. Rogers's homeroom?" she asked in a soft voice.

"Are you Amber Sweeny?" Ms. Rogers asked. The girl nodded.

"*I'm in love!*" Alex groaned and the kids around him chuckled.

"Please take a seat," Ms. Rogers said. "I was just reading a bulletin from Principal Blanco regarding treatment of the new sixth-graders, but I don't think it's something you'll need to worry about."

Amber Sweeny smiled slightly and quickly took a seat . . . right next to me.

For a moment the class was totally silent. I glanced around the room and saw that almost everyone was staring at Amber with the same starstruck expression.

As if a goddess had just entered our midst.

Then I felt someone poke me in the ribs. It was Alex.

"Say something to her," he whispered, just loud enough for the kids around us to hear.

"Get lost," I whispered back.

"Chicken?" he taunted.

17

I felt my face turn red, but didn't say anything. I was pretty sure Amber could hear Alex, too.

"*Bawk, bawk, bawk,*" Alex started to make chicken sounds. The kids around us started to giggle.

"*You* say something to her," I whispered back.

"I would, but I'm not sitting next to her," Alex replied.

"Jake, what's going on back there?" Ms. Rogers asked.

I quickly turned around and faced the front. The kids around us were still giggling. I grinned nervously and felt my face turn even redder.

"Uh, nothing, Ms. Rogers," I said.

Brinnggg . . . The bell rang and it was time to go to our first class. Everyone got up. I could feel Ms. Rogers's eyes on me as I headed for the door.

"Jake?" she said, just as I was about to leave the room.

"Uh, yeah?" I paused.

"I'd like to have a word with you."

The other kids gave me looks and smirked.

"But I'll be late for my next class," I said.

"I can give you a pass," Ms. Rogers said. "I'm a teacher, remember? Or maybe you've forgotten."

It was obvious from her tone that she was mad. Alex came by and patted me on the shoulder.

"Catch you later, Sir Jake," he said quietly and went out, leaving me to face Ms. Rogers alone.

4

Ms. Rogers leaned against her desk with her arms crossed.

"Something's changed," she said.

I tried to imagine what Alex would say. Probably something cool like, "Oh, yeah?" or "Tell me about it." But somehow, I couldn't quite get myself to say anything like that.

"Do you know what it is?" Ms. Rogers asked.

I had a feeling I knew, but I shook my head anyway.

"It's you," she said. "And do you know what about you has changed?"

"Uh, I got a little taller over the summer?"

Ms. Rogers shook her head.

"Well, uh, I've noticed a couple of whiskers on my upper lip," I said.

Ms. Rogers smiled slightly. "No, Jake. What's changed is that you're starting to get into trouble again. Remember in sixth grade when I used to call you my favorite troublemaker?"

I nodded.

"Well, what seemed cute and funny then doesn't seem so cute and funny now," she said. "You're two years older and it's time to grow up."

I looked down at the floor. She was starting to sound like my sister and my parents.

"May I give you a word of advice?" Ms. Rogers asked.

I shrugged.

"Find a new friend."

The rest of the morning was the typical first-day stuff: information about fire drills, lectures on good behavior and respecting each other, explanations of grading procedures, and so on.

The high point of the morning was gym. Mr. Cooper, the gym teacher, said we had to wash ourselves and our gym uniforms frequently because our body chemistry was changing in ways that teachers and other students might find offensive.

"Tell me, Sir Jake," said Alex after gym, as we walked to lunch. "Hast thou ever heard a more original way of saying we had B-O?"

"Forsooth, I have not," I replied with a grin.

We walked into the cafeteria. The lunch line was pretty long, so we cut in front.

"Hey, what d'ya think you're doing?" a kid behind us asked.

"Exercising our eighth-grade privileges, peasant," Alex replied.

"That's not allowed," the kid said. "I'm gonna tell Principal Blanco."

"So be it," Alex said with a shrug.

The kid turned to go, but another kid grabbed his arm. "I wouldn't if I were you."

"Why not?" asked the first kid.

"They'll make sure you pay for the rest of the year," the other kid said.

"But it's not fair," complained the first kid.

"Don't worry," said the other kid. "You'll get your chance when you're in eighth grade."

Alex and I smiled at each other as we slid our trays down the silver railing toward the lunch ladies. It felt good to be on the top of the heap. It felt good to be feared.

The menu for the first day was always cheeseburgers and fries. It was a Burp-It-Up tradition. Moments later we came out of the lunch line with our trays and looked around for a table.

"Check it out, Sir Jake." Alex nodded toward Amber Sweeny, who sat alone eating a salad. "Dost thou think Princess Amber would like company?"

"Certainly, Sir Alex, go right ahead," I replied.

"Well, I meant . . ." Alex hesitated. "We could go together."

"Well, uh . . ." The idea of sitting with her

made me pretty nervous. I had the feeling Alex was nervous about it, too. Just then Ms. Rogers, who was on lunch duty, stopped by the table where Amber was sitting and started to chat with her.

"Too late," Alex muttered. "The evil witch has foiled our plans."

"Perhaps tomorrow we will sit with the princess," I suggested.

"Yes, tomorrow," Alex agreed.

We headed toward an empty table. Out of the corner of my eye I noticed two other kids heading for it, too. We all got there at the same time and put our trays down. Looking up, I saw that the other two guys were my old friends, Andy Kent and Josh Hopka.

It looked like Andy had gotten a little taller over the summer and had cut his black hair short. Josh had thinned down a little. His face was tan and full of freckles.

We all nodded at each other and sat down. I sat across from Alex, and Andy sat across from Josh. I could feel their eyes on me.

"So how was your summer, Jake?" Josh asked.

"Okay," I said, picking up a soggy fry and biting into it. "How was yours?"

"Okay," Josh said. "Didn't see you around much."

"Yeah." What else could I do but nod?

Josh turned back to Andy. "Guess Jake's got a new friend," he said loudly.

"Yeah, so he doesn't need his old friends anymore," Andy replied, picking up his burger.

"I hear they call themselves the Knights of Wedgy," Josh said. "The word is they did a real number on some new kid this morning."

Alex bristled. "Are these guys bothering you?" he asked me loudly.

"No." I quickly shook my head. The last thing I wanted to do was get into a fight with my old friends. Actually, I was kind of surprised that they were so peeved about not seeing me over the summer.

Meanwhile, Andy took a big bite of his cheeseburger and started to chew.

"*Blech!*" Without warning he bent over and spit the cheeseburger back onto his tray.

"Gross!" Alex shouted, jumping up from the table.

"What happened?" I asked.

"I think he hurled," said Alex.

"I didn't hurl," Andy said, wiping his mouth with a napkin. He pointed at the half-chewed yellow-and-brown glob on the tray. "That's the worst thing I ever tasted."

"Well, cover it up or something," Josh said. "I'm getting sick just looking at it."

Andy took the bun from his cheeseburger and

covered the glob. "Forget it. I just lost my appetite."

Alex and I looked at each other. Andy may have lost his appetite, but we still had ours. We sat down again and picked up our cheeseburgers, but neither of us took a bite.

"You go first," Alex said.

"No, *you*," I said.

"I dare you."

"Drop dead."

"He will if he eats that thing," Andy said. "I swear, it tastes like it was left over from last year."

"I'll do it if you'll do it," Alex dared me.

"Promise?" I asked.

"You guys are nuts," said Andy.

"Maybe it was just *your* burger, Andy," Josh said.

Alex and I brought the cheeseburgers up to our noses and sniffed them. Alex wrinkled his nose.

"How does it smell?" Josh asked.

"Like regular mystery meat to me," I said.

"They must have put something on it to mask the smell," Andy said. "I'm warning you, guys, you eat that thing and the only way you'll leave this cafeteria is by Medivac."

My stomach growled hungrily. I knew if I was hungry, Alex and Josh were hungry, too.

"What do you think?" Alex asked.

"Maybe Josh is right and Andy's was the only bad one," I said.

"I say we all bite at once," Alex said.

Josh and I glanced at each other and nodded. We all slowly opened our mouths and put the cheeseburgers in, but none of us bit.

"Guffaffed, buff." Josh tried to talk with the cheeseburger bun in his mouth.

I turned to Andy. *"Whuff fee fay?"* I asked with my bun still in my mouth.

"I think he said, go ahead, bite," Andy said.

I turned to Alex. *"Whuff afout yoo?"*

"What about you?" Andy interpreted.

"I fill fen yoof foo," Alex replied.

"He says he will when you do," Andy said.

"Fofay," I said. *"Uh fun, an uh foo, and uh fee!"* Josh and I both bit down at the same time.

"Blech!" The horrible taste of spoiled meat filled my mouth. Josh and I spit out our bites.

"That's the worst!" I cried.

"It's rancid!" Josh quickly sipped his orange drink to get rid of the taste.

"You dorks!" Alex laughed and put down his untouched burger.

"Hey!" Josh said angrily. "We all agreed to bite at the same time. It was your idea."

"Give me a break," Alex said with a big smile.

Josh picked up his tray. "Come on, Andy, let's get something else to eat." He and Andy got up.

Josh looked back at me. "Great friend, Jake," he said sarcastically.

Alex and I watched them leave.

"You really used to hang out with those two?" he asked.

I nodded.

Alex shook his head. "Chumps."

5

We ate potato chips and ice cream for lunch and then kicked the seventh-graders off the basketball court and played H-O-R-S-E until the bell.

Next class was science with Mr. Dirksen, who we'd last had in sixth grade. We used to call him Mr. *Dork*sen, but after he and I accidentally switched bodies, he'd become a much cooler teacher.

As we walked into the classroom, I saw that Andy and Josh had just arrived. Mr. Dirksen was standing at the blackboard writing something. Only, he didn't look like Mr. Dirksen anymore.

"Whoa! Mr. Dirksen, you got hair!" Andy cried.

Mr. Dirksen ran his hand over his his head, which used to be bald, but now had straight brown hair.

"Had a transplant," he said. "What do you think?"

"Did Ms. Rogers make you do it?" Josh asked.

"She said she didn't care either way," Mr. Dirksen said, "but secretly I think she likes it."

Brinnnggg. . . . The bell rang.

"All right, everyone," Mr. Dirksen said, handing out double sheets of paper. "Take your seats. Hurry, we have lots to do."

Alex and I sat down in the back of the room. Josh and Andy sat in the front. Mr. Dirksen started to close the door when Amber Sweeny hurried in.

"Sorry I'm late," she said breathlessly.

"Just find a seat," Mr. Dirksen said.

There was an empty seat next to me, and Amber sat down in it. She gave me a brief smile, and I smiled back nervously.

I felt a finger poke me in the ribs. "Now's your chance," Alex whispered.

"Chill, dude," I whispered back.

Meanwhile in front, Andy held up the pages Mr. Dirksen had just given out. "Uh, excuse me, but this looks an awful lot like a test."

"It is," Mr. Dirksen replied.

"What?" "Huh?" "Is he serious?" All around the room kids expressed their disbelief. I looked down at the test, which had something to do with naming the parts of a cell. Amber turned and gave me a puzzled look. It was the perfect chance to say something to her, but the words seemed to get caught in my throat.

"You can't give us a test on the first day of school," said Josh.

"Why not?" Mr. Dirksen asked.

"Because no one's had time to study," Andy said.

"A test is supposed to measure your knowledge in a certain area," Mr. Dirksen replied calmly. "I simply want to see how much you know."

"Great," Andy groaned. "So we'll all start off the year with an F."

"On the contrary," Mr. Dirksen said. "You'll start off the year with a good idea of what you're going to study."

"But it's not fair," said a girl named Julia Sax.

"What isn't fair about it?" Mr. Dirksen replied.

"We had no advance warning," said Julia.

"Yeah, this is really gonna mess up our GPAs," said Josh.

"It won't harm your grade point averages at all," said Mr. Dirksen.

"It won't?" Andy frowned.

"I'll grade it, but it's not going to count," Mr. Dirksen said with a big smile.

All around the room kids let out big sighs of relief.

"Why didn't you tell us that in the first place?" Andy asked.

"No one gave me a chance to," Mr. Dirksen explained.

Everybody had a big laugh, and then we spent the rest of the period trying to do the test. After class, Alex and I stopped at our lockers to dump some books.

"What a jerk," Alex said.

"Who?" I said.

"Mr. Dirksen."

"Why?" I said, surprised. "He said the test wouldn't count."

"Yeah." Alex nodded. "That's what he *said*, but you'll see."

Just then Amber Sweeny walked by and went down the hall.

"You had the perfect chance to talk to her," Alex said.

"What was I supposed to say?" I asked, closing my locker.

"You could have said a million things," Alex said. "Like what a jerk Mr. Dirksen was. Or how hot-looking she is. Or just about anything."

"I didn't see you say anything to her," I said as we started down the hall.

"I wasn't sitting next to her," said Alex. Then he added, "Hey, look who's coming."

Down the hall I caught a glimpse of a familiar-looking blond head being jostled in the crowd. A moment later we came face-to-face with Ollie. He stared up at us through his glasses.

"Why it's Dweeb Ollie of Ohio," Alex said with

a sinister grin. "You get to homeroom on time this morning?"

Ollie shook his head. "You got me really lost."

"Aw, isn't that too bad?" Alex pouted.

"I don't want to be late for my next class." Ollie started around Alex.

"Not so fast, Dweeb Ollie." Alex grabbed the strap of his backpack and stopped him. Then he looked at me. "Any teachers?"

I quickly looked up and down the hall. All I saw were kids. "Nope."

"Excellent." Alex started to tug Ollie. "It's very important that you learn about our school, Dweeb Ollie of Ohio. And one place you must get to know is . . . the girls' room."

"Oh, no!" Ollie gasped and tried to squirm out of Alex's grip. But Alex kicked the girls' room door open with his foot and pushed Ollie inside.

"Hey! Let me out!" Ollie's muffled shouts came through the wooden door. Alex held the door closed while I watched for teachers.

Thunk! Thunk! Thunk! Ollie pounded desperately on the inside of the girls' room door. "Come on, guys! Let me out! *Please!*"

Out in the hall, Alex smiled fiendishly as a bunch of kids stopped to see what the commotion was about.

"What's going on?" someone asked.

31

"I think he's got some kid trapped in the girls' room," said someone else.

Suddenly another voice joined Ollie's inside the girls' room. "Let him out, for Pete's sake."

It was a girl's voice. Alex quickly let go of the door. It swung open, and Ollie hurried out and sped down the hall without even looking at us. Alex and I nudged each other and chuckled.

Then Amber Sweeny stepped out of the girls' room.

Alex and I stopped smiling.

The crowd around us grew quiet.

Amber fixed us with her piercing green eyes.

"Grow up," she said, and walked away.

6

My parents usually didn't get home until around 7:30, so Jessica cooked dinner every night.

"How was school, Mr. Big Shot?" she asked that night as she dumped a package of spaghetti into a pot of water boiling on the stove.

"Okay." I sat slumped at the kitchen table. The memory of Amber's put-down was still ringing painfully in my ears.

"How many sixth-graders did you wedgy?" she asked.

I blinked as I realized that besides the shoe-wedgy of Dweeb Ollie of Ohio that morning, we hadn't wedgied anyone. "Uh, none."

Jessica looked surprised. "What happened to all your plans?"

"We did most of 'em," I said.

"Boy, you must've felt like big, tough eighth-graders pushing all those little kids around," Jessica said snidely.

"Look, just drop it, okay?"

Jessica shrugged and started to heat up the tomato sauce. Being a vegetarian, she never put any meat in it. "Remember that fire this morning?"

"Huh?" It took me a second to remember. "Oh, yeah, what about it?"

"It was a few blocks over," she said. "A new family just moved in. I heard they left the toaster oven on. There's hardly anything left."

"Wow, cool," I said. "Want to go over there after dinner and take a look?"

"I can't," Jessica said. "I have to read a whole chapter of biology, plus do geometry and world history."

"Too bad."

My sister gave me a look of utter disgust. "What's happened to you?"

"I don't know, what?" I asked, bewildered.

"When did you become to kind of the person who thinks it's cool when someone's house burns down?"

7

DAY TWO

Beep . . . beep . . . beep! The alarm went off and I opened my eyes. It was time to get up and go to school.

Jessica was in the kitchen having her usual bowl of granola when I came in.

"Ready?" she asked as I got the box of Pop-Tarts out of the cupboard.

"For what?" I asked, tearing the box open.

"It's the first day of school, remember?"

"What are you talking about?"I asked.

Jessica rolled her eyes. "Get a grip, Jake."

"*You* get a grip," I said. "The first day was yesterday."

Jessica stared at me like I was crazy. "I went to the pool with Cathy yesterday."

I stared back at Jessica like *she* was crazy. Then I looked down at the box of chocolate Pop-Tarts.

35

Why was I tearing open a new box? I'd just opened one yesterday. I looked in the cupboard for the open box, but it wasn't there.

"Hey, what'd you do with my Pop-Tarts?" I asked.

"They're in your hand."

"Not these," I said. "I opened a box yesterday. Where are they?"

"Don't look at me," my sister said. "I didn't touch them."

"Yeah, right." I didn't believe her. Then I noticed something else strange. "Why are you wearing the same clothes as yesterday?"

"What?" Jessica scowled at me.

"That's what you wore to school yesterday," I said. "Aren't you worried some of your politically correct friends might object?"

Jessica stared at me again like I was crazy. "Are you feeling okay?"

"I was until now," I said. "I mean, when you were in eighth grade, didn't Mr. Cooper give you that dumb lecture about how your body chemistry was changing in ways that teachers and other students might find offensive?"

"Yes," said my sister. "How did you know about that?"

"Because he gave it yesterday."

"He couldn't have, Jake. There was no school yesterday."

"Of course there was," I said. "You wore those clothes."

"I just got this top at the mall last night," Jessica said. "What's with you?"

"What's with me?" I asked. "Hey, I'm not the one pretending today's the first day of school."

"It *is* the first day."

Suddenly I figured out what she was up to. "Very funny, Jessica. Good joke."

"It's not a joke," my sister said. "I don't know what you're talking about."

"Yeah, right." The conversation was getting nowhere. I turned and looked out the kitchen window. Ollie was already at the bus stop.

"Do you believe it?" I said. "Dweeb Ollie's early again."

"Who?" Jessica asked.

"Ollie," I said. "Remember yesterday morning? That blond kid who got to the bus stop early? Well, his name's Oliver, but Alex dubbed him Dweeb Ollie of Ohio."

Jessica didn't answer. She just stared at me like I was completely out of my gourd.

"Oh, right," I said with a smile. "Now you don't remember *him* either."

Suddenly the town's fire siren began to blast — *Whaaaaa-O-Whaaaaa-O-Whaaaaa!* . . .

That's strange, I thought. *Two mornings in a row?*

A moment later a car horn honked.

"That's Cathy," Jessica said. "Her sister's giving us a ride to school. Want to come?"

Suddenly I felt a very weird sensation. Like major *déjà vu*. Weren't those the exact same words my sister had used the day before?

"Jake?"

"Huh?" I looked at her, puzzled.

"Are you okay?"

"Uh, yeah, sure."

"Cathy's sister's giving us a ride to school. You can come if you want."

"Uh, that's okay," I said. "I told Alex I'd meet him at the bus stop."

"Of course." Jessica smiled snidely as she left. "You're Sir Jake, a Knight of Wedgy now. It's time to start your little reign of terror."

A few moments later I left the house, feeling kind of weird.

Eeeeiiiiirrrrnnnn! Eeeeiiiiirrrrnnnn! The big red-and-silver pumper truck raced past, going down Bay Drive with its lights flashing. A couple of seconds later another fire truck shot past. Once again it looked like they were heading for a house a couple of blocks away.

That strange feeling grew stronger. Almost like it was yesterday all over again.

By the time I got to the bus stop, Alex and the

other kids had also arrived. Once again, Alex was wearing a black T-shirt.

When he saw me, he raised his hand. "Sir Jake, dude!"

I just stared at him. *What was going on?*

Alex frowned. "I said, Sir Jake, dude!"

I gave him the high five and glanced around at the other kids. They were all giving us the same scared looks and wearing the same clothes as the day before!

"Are we the Knights of Wedgy?" Alex asked.

"Yeah, sure," I said and turned to Ollie. Once again he gave me that awestruck, wide-eyed look. He was wearing the same blue short-sleeve shirt and khaki slacks as yesterday.

"Remember me?" I asked.

Ollie shook his head.

"Come on, Ollie," I said. "Me and Alex made you miss the bus yesterday. Then we got you lost at school and pushed you into the girls' room."

Ollie looked at me like I was crazy. "There was no school yesterday. And how do you know my name?"

"Yeah, what's with you, Jake?" Alex asked.

They were all staring at me — the same way Jessica had.

"Uh, nothing," I said.

"Good," Alex said. "Are we bad?"

I nodded.

"Do we wedgy?"

Again I nodded. Something totally bizarre was going on. Just as he had the day before, Alex turned to the little group around us and told them to stand at attention.

"What if we don't?" Robbie Bayuk asked again.

"You'll get wedgied," Alex threatened again.

"Wait a minute," I said. "Didn't anybody here go to school yesterday?"

Alex turned and gave me a peculiar look. "Why?"

"Because it was the — " I started to say "the first day of school," but then I caught myself. I knew they'd all gone to school the day before. I'd *seen* them go to school.

Everyone except Ollie got in the row.

Alex peered down at him. "What manner of creature is this?"

It *had* to be some kind of joke.

Alex turned to me. "Sir Jake, I asked you what manner of creature is this."

"It's a Dweeb Ollie of Ohio," I said. "You know that from yesterday."

Alex frowned. Then he turned to Ollie. "What's your name?"

"Well, my name's Oliver and I *am* from Ohio," the kid said. "And people do call me Ollie."

Alex looked back at me and grinned. "Very good, mind reader."

I didn't know what to say. This was impossible.

It couldn't be happening. And yet it was. Right before my eyes, everything was happening just as it had the day before. I listened in amazement as Ollie said he didn't know what a wedgy was. Then, just like the day before, Alex gave him a shoe wedgy and sent him around the block.

"Like a true dweeb," Alex muttered. Then he turned to me. "Hast thou any gum, Sir Jake?"

Gum? I'd had a pack yesterday, but I'd finished it at school.

"Sorry." I shook my head.

Alex frowned and stuck his hand into the pocket of my T-shirt. "What's this?" He pulled out a pack of Juicy Fruit.

"Uh . . ." I was sure I'd finished it the day before.

Alex pulled a stick out and put the pack back into my pocket. "I am surprised at you, Sir Jake. We Knights of Wedgy share everything."

I knew for a fact that I'd finished that gum the day before. Now I watched in total amazement as Alex went across the street and moved Mr. MacDowell's garbage can into the driveway again. Mr. MacDowell backed into it, and Alex made the kids clap.

Something totally and extremely weird was going on. The day before was all happening all over again! And no one seemed to know it except me!

8

At school I did my combination and opened my locker. The afternoon before, I'd left some books in it. But now it was completely empty.

"Uh, Sir Jake?"

I turned and found Alex holding the letter his locker combination had come on.

"You just did your combination without looking at your letter," he said.

"Oh, uh, yeah," I stammered.

Alex squinted at me. "You *memorized* it?"

"Uh, I guess."

"Listen, Sir Jake," Alex said, stepping close and speaking in a low voice. "Only dorks memorize their locker combination before the first day of school. Now I'm willing to pretend it didn't happen, but get real, dude."

Brinnnggg! The homeroom bell rang. Alex and I were just about to go in when we heard the sound of rapid footsteps coming down the hall toward us. It was Ollie, red-faced and out of breath.

Once again he couldn't find his homeroom. Once again Alex winked at me and sent him on a wild-goose chase. Then we went into our homeroom.

I think I was in a daze while Ms. Rogers read the bulletin from Principal Blanco. Every single person was wearing exactly what they'd worn the day before. And nobody complained that she'd read the bulletin yesterday.

What did it mean? Why was it happening?

Once again Alex made his wisecracks, and asked about nature wedgies and Melvins.

Then the door opened and Amber Sweeny came in, and everyone stared at her with the same star-struck expression. Alex made the same wise-cracks. Then the kids around us chuckled, and I felt him poke me in the ribs.

"Say something to her," he whispered, just loud enough for everyone to hear.

"Why don't you?" I whispered back.

"I would, but I'm not sitting next to her."

"Hey, no problem." I got out of my seat and stood up.

Suddenly the whole class was staring at me. And I realized something. Everyone was going through the first day again, but I didn't have to do the same things I did the day before.

"What is it, Jake?" Ms. Rogers asked.

"Oh, uh . . ." I felt my face start to burn with embarrassment. What was I supposed to say? "I, uh, have to go."

"The bell hasn't rung yet," Ms. Rogers replied, looking up at the clock.

Brinnggg . . . The bell rang. Everyone got up.

"What's with you?" Alex whispered in my ear, as we started toward the door.

How could I explain? I was just about to leave the room when Ms. Rogers said, "Jake?"

"Uh, yeah?" I paused.

"I'd like to have a word with you."

The other kids in the class were giving me looks and smirking. The memory of yesterday was still fresh in my mind.

Alex patted me on the shoulder. "Catch you later, Sir Jake."

Ms. Rogers waited until everyone had left the room.

"I'm sorry, Ms. Rogers," I said. "I didn't mean to interrupt."

Ms. Rogers looked puzzled. "Interrupt what?"

"Well, you know, homeroom."

"I didn't think you had," she said.

"Huh?" I didn't understand. "But that's why you asked me to stay, isn't it?"

"No." She shook her head. "I have some news I wanted to tell you."

"Oh, uh, yeah. Congratulations," I said.

"You know?" Ms. Rogers looked surprised. "How?"

"You . . . uh . . . er . . . I heard yesterday."

"But we just got back last night," she said. "It

44

was such a last-minute thing that we didn't have time to tell anyone."

"Oh, uh . . . that's right. I didn't hear it." I pointed at her finger. "I saw the ring."

Ms. Rogers and I both looked down at the gold band on her finger.

"Well, you're extremely observant," she said, giving me a skeptical look. "Jake, are you all right?"

"Uh, why do you ask?"

"Well, you seem a little . . . off."

I forced a smile on my face. "Must be because it's the first day of school, huh?"

Ms. Rogers smiled back. "Yes, I guess that's it. Now you better go or you'll be late for your next class."

The rest of the day went the same way. I had to be really careful not to let anyone know that I'd already been through it once. Otherwise they'd ask too many questions that I couldn't answer. Instead I did everything exactly the way I had the day before. At lunch, Alex and I talked about sitting with Amber, but used Ms. Rogers as an excuse to chicken out. I even let Alex trick me and Josh into biting into the rancid cheeseburgers. Later on I acted surprised by Mr. Dirksen's test, and watched for teachers while Alex pushed Ollie into the girls' room, knowing that Amber Sweeny would come out and tell us to grow up.

That night, Jessica made the same vegetarian spaghetti. "So how was school, Mr. Big Shot?"

"Weird," I said.

"Weird?" It was obvious that wasn't what she'd expected to hear.

"Uh-huh."

"How many sixth-graders did you wedgy?" she asked.

"None."

Once again Jessica looked surprised. "What happened to all your plans?"

I just shrugged. What good would it do to tell her how I'd gone through the first day of school two days in a row? She wouldn't believe me in a million years. And if I *really* insisted it had happened, she'd probably tell my parents and they'd probably send me to a shrink or something.

It just wasn't worth it. All I could do was pray that tomorrow would be different.

9

DAY THREE

Beep . . . beep . . . beep! I opened my eyes and looked around. Was it the same, or was it different? I jumped out of bed and went out into the upstairs hall wearing a pair of pajama shorts.

Jessica's door was closed. I knocked.

"Jake?" she called through the door.

"Yeah, can I come in?"

"No, I'm not dressed. What is it?"

"What are you wearing?"

"What?"

"I asked what you're wearing today."

"I just told you, I'm not wearing anything yet."

"Yeah, but what will you wear when you're wearing something?" I asked.

"Are you feeling okay?"

"Just tell me."

"Well, I guess I'll wear my black skirt and my new black top."

I started to get a sinking feeling. "The one you got at the mall last night?"

"That's right. Why?"

"Is today the first day of school?"

"Oh, come on, Jake. You know it is."

My knees felt weak. I slid down the wall and sat on the carpet in the upstairs hall, overcome by a horrible realization: *It was the first day again! I was trapped in the first day of school!* Jessica opened her door a little and peeked down at me.

"What's with you?" she asked.

"Remember how Mr. Dirksen and I switched bodies in sixth grade?" I said. "Well, it's happened again."

"You're Mr. Dirksen?" Jessica started to cover herself up.

"No, I'm Jake." Then I explained how I wasn't trapped in someone else's body this time. I was trapped in a day.

"You're trapped in the first day of school?" Jessica looked at me like I was crazy.

"You went to the pool yesterday with Cathy, right?"

"Yes."

"Well, I went to school," I said. "And the day before that, too."

Now Jessica gave me a suspicious look. "Are

you trying to say you've already done the first day of school so you don't have to go today?"

"No," I said. "I'll go. I mean, I guess I have to."

"You better. I don't think Mom and Dad would believe that you skipped school today because you'd already done it."

"But, I just want to know if you believe me," I said.

"I don't know," Jessica said. "I mean, what difference does it make? You still have to go to school today. And I'd get dressed if I were you, or you're going to be late."

I got up and went back into my room and got dressed. It might not have made a difference to my sister. But it made a big difference to me.

Later, Jessica gave me a funny look when I came into the kitchen.

"Are you okay?" she asked.

"No," I said, opening the cupboard. The unopened box of chocolate Pop-Tarts was there again, but I was getting kind of sick of them. Instead I got a bowl and filled it with granola.

"What are you doing?" Jessica asked.

"I'm having breakfast."

"You never eat granola."

"I do now," I said. "I've had chocolate Pop-Tarts for two mornings in a row and I'm getting sick of them."

"The Pop-Tarts box isn't even open, Jake."

"I know," I said. "But I opened it yesterday and the day before, too."

Jessica gave me that look again — like I'd lost my marbles. "Jake, if you opened it yesterday morning, why isn't it still open this morning?"

"Because this is yesterday all over again," I tried to explain.

My sister didn't say anything. She just stared at me.

"Okay," I said, carrying my bowl of granola over to the kitchen counter and pointing out the window. "See the bus stop?"

Jessica got up and came over. "Yes."

"In about a minute a kid with blond hair is going to show up. He'll be wearing a blue shirt, khaki pants, white tennis shoes, and carrying a green backpack. His name's Oliver but everyone calls him Ollie and he just moved here from Ohio."

The words were barely out of my mouth when Ollie arrived and looked around like he wasn't certain he was in the right place.

Jessica gave me a shocked look. "How did you know that?"

"Because he's done it for the past two days."

"Why?"

"I already told you," I said. "Because it's been the first day of school for the past two days."

My sister picked up her bowl of granola and

moved away, looking at me like I'd just escaped from the nut house.

"What are you doing?" I asked.

"I'm worried about you, Jake."

"I'm not crazy," I said. "I just told you what would happen and it happened."

Jessica nodded warily.

"I know you find it hard to believe," I said. "But this is the third first day of school in a row. Except I'm the only one who knows it."

"Is this a joke?" Jessica asked.

"I wish."

"Why are you telling me this?"

"Are you serious?" Now I looked at her like *she* she was crazy. "Wouldn't you tell people if it was happening to you?"

"I . . . I don't know," she said uncertainly.

Suddenly I realized what time it was. "The town fire siren is going to go off."

Whaaaaa-O-Whaaaaa-O-Whaaaa!

"How did you know that?" Jessica gasped, staring at me with wide eyes.

"I've told you five times," I said. "Better get your stuff. Cathy's sister is pulling into the driveway."

Jessica spun around and pulled back the curtain on the window that faced the driveway. Outside, a red car pulled up. She let go of the curtain and stared at me again.

"I don't understand," she said.

"Neither do I," I said.

"What are you going to do?"

"Go to school. I mean, what other choice do I have?"

The fire engines raced past as I walked down to the bus stop. Everyone was there again. Alex and I greeted each other. Then he picked on Ollie and made him run around the block.

"Like a true dweeb," Alex muttered. Then he turned to me.

"Here you go." I handed him a stick of Juicy Fruit.

Alex looked surprised. "How did you know I was going to ask for a piece of gum?"

"Teenage intuition," I said with a shrug.

10

We got to school, put our stuff in our lockers, sent Ollie on his wild-goose chase, and went in to homeroom. Then I had an idea.

"Hey, Alex, why don't you sit here?" I said, gesturing to the seat I'd sat in for the past two days.

"Why?" Alex asked.

"Why not?"

"Okay." Alex sat down and Ms. Rogers read the bulletin from Principal Blanco. Then the door opened and Amber Sweeny came in. Just as I expected, she took the seat next to Alex.

While the rest of the class stared at Amber, Alex glanced at me with wide eyes and mouthed the word, "Wow!"

"Say something to her," I whispered.

Alex glanced at Amber and shrugged. "Like what?"

"I don't know," I whispered. "You're not chicken, are you?"

"Jake?" Ms. Rogers called from the front of the room.

I quickly turned around. "Sorry."

"That's better." Ms. Rogers smiled. Then the bell rang and she asked me to stay after so she could tell me the news about her and Mr. Dirksen. I felt like I was getting into a routine.

Everything went the same until lunch, when Alex and I invoked eighth-grade privileges and cut to the front of the line. As we slid our trays along the silver rail, I remembered what we were in for.

"Cheeseburgers, boys?" asked a lunch lady wearing a hair net and plastic gloves.

"Sure," said Alex.

"No, thanks." I picked up a bag of chips and an ice cream instead.

"Health food, Sir Jake?" Alex smirked.

"Right, Sir Alex." I winked back.

We came out of the lunch line and saw Amber sitting alone.

"Check it out, Sir Jake," Alex said. "Dost thou think Princess Amber would like company?"

"Most certainly, Sir Alex," I replied, and started toward her, wondering what Alex would do.

Alex hesitated. "Art thou serious, Sir Jake?"

I stopped and looked back at him. "Why, of course, Sir Alex. Was it not your idea?"

"Well, uh . . ." Alex looked to his left. "Uh-oh."

"What is it, Sir Alex?" I asked.

"The evil witch approaches," he said, nodding at Ms. Rogers.

"So?" I asked.

"I have a bad feeling." Alex waited until Ms. Rogers stopped to chat with Amber. "Just as I thought."

I stared at Alex in amazement. "How did you know?"

"How did I know what?" Alex asked back.

"That Ms. Rogers was going to talk to Amber?"

"I didn't," Alex said. "It was just a guess."

I didn't believe him. "Listen, Alex, you can tell me. It's okay. It's not my first day of school either. I just thought I was the only one."

"What are you talking about?" Alex asked.

"I'm talking about going to school yesterday. That's how you knew Ms. Rogers was going to talk to Amber."

"You're really losing it, Jake. There was no school yesterday."

"You sure?" I squinted at him.

Alex shook his head. "Time for a serious reality check, dude. And anyway, the evil witch has foiled our plans."

I felt incredibly disappointed. For a moment I was sure Alex was going through the first day of school again just like me. But now it looked like he'd simply made a lucky guess.

Once again we arrived at the table just as Josh and Andy got there. We all sat down.

"Hey, guys, long time no see," I said in a friendly tone.

Josh and Andy gave each other surprised looks.

"So how was your summer?" I asked.

"Okay," Josh said. "Didn't see much of you."

"Yeah, I don't know what happened," I said. "Guess it went really fast."

"I guess." Josh looked a little puzzled.

Andy picked up his burger.

"I'd be careful if I were you," I said.

"Why?" Andy asked.

"I hear the burgers are a little gross."

Andy frowned and sniffed the burger. "Smells okay to me."

"They put something on it to mask the smell," I said. "I'm just warning you."

Andy took a small bite and chewed it.

"*Blech!*" He spit it out. "He's right. It's totally bogus!"

Now Josh and Alex looked down at their cheeseburgers.

"It's not just his, guys," I warned. "It's all of them."

Josh wrinkled his forehead. "How do you know, Jake?"

"Believe me," I said. "I've been there. I know."

*   *   *

After lunch we went to Mr. Dirksen's room. Once again, I made sure Alex had the seat I'd had on the two previous days. Mr. Dirksen was handing out the test when Amber Sweeny hurried in and took the seat next to Alex.

This time Alex didn't glance over at me. I guess he knew what I'd say. I nudged him anyway.

"Back off, Jake!" he hissed.

Some brave guy, huh?

"Now's your chance to say something to her," I whispered.

"I said, drop it!" Alex hissed again.

I could have kept it up, but somehow I didn't get the same charge out of goofing on Alex that he seemed to get out of goofing on me.

Meanwhile, Andy had just pointed out that Mr. Dirksen's handout looked an awful lot like a test. Just as he had on the last two days, Mr. Dirksen told us that he only wanted to see how much we knew and that we wouldn't get graded on it.

I raised my hand. "Then what's the point? You know that we don't know this stuff."

"Some of you may know some of it," Mr. Dirksen replied. "I want to use this as a baseline comparison for the tests I'll give you later in the year."

Then I got a funny idea. "What would happen if one of us aced the test?"

"I guess it would show that you knew the material," Mr. Dirksen replied.

"Wouldn't that mean that we wouldn't need to take this class this year?" I asked.

"I'll tell you what," Mr. Dirksen said with a smile. "Since I know for a fact that no one in this classroom could possibly ace this test without studying — and being this is the first day of school, none of you have studied — if it makes you happy, I'd say yes. Anyone who aces the test will not have to take my class this year."

"And we'll still get a good grade?" Josh asked.

"You'll get an *A* for the year and you won't have to show up for a single class," Mr. Dirksen said with a smug smile.

"All right!" I pumped my arm triumphantly.

"What are you so excited about?" Alex asked. "There's no way you're gonna ace it."

"Hey," I said. "You never know."

We took the test. Mr. Dirksen said he'd look them over before the end of the day and he'd let us know if anyone aced it. After class, Alex and I stopped at our lockers to dump some books. Then Amber Sweeny walked by.

"How come you didn't talk to her?" I asked Alex.

"I was gonna, but then you started talking about the test and I forgot."

That's a good one, I thought as we started down the hall.

A moment later we came face-to-face with Ollie. He stared up at us through his glasses.

58

"Why it's Dweeb Ollie of Ohio," Alex said. "You get to homeroom on time this morning?"

For the third day in a row Ollie told us how lost he'd gotten that morning. Then Alex dragged him toward the girls' room.

"Oh, no!" Ollie gasped and tried to squirm out of Alex's grip. Once again I was supposed to watch for teachers. Only this time, I "thought" I saw one.

"I think someone's coming," I said just before Alex could push Ollie into the girls' room. Alex let go of the sixth-grader, who quickly disappeared into the crowd.

"Where?" Alex asked, squinting down the hall. "I don't see anyone."

"Gee, you're right," I said. Then the girls' room door opened and Amber came out. She gave us a brief smile and headed down the hall.

It felt good not to be put down for once.

That day after school, I was sitting in my room, studying the parts of a cell, when Jessica knocked and came in.

"What are you doing?" she asked.

"Studying."

My sister's jaw dropped. "You? Study?"

"Sure. I've got a big science test tomorrow."

"On the *second* day of school?"

I shook my head. "Remember this morning? It'll probably be the first day all over again."

"So what am I going to do for the rest of today?" she asked.

"Well, you'll probably start your homework before dinner because you have to read a whole chapter of biology, plus geometry and world history. Then you'll make that disgusting vegetarian spaghetti for supper. Then you'll do more homework. Oh, wait. Before you do that, you'll tell me about the fire this morning. It was the home of some people who just moved in. They left the toaster oven on."

"How do you know all this?" Jessica's eyes widened and she brought her hand to her mouth.

"I keep telling you, I've done the first day of school three days in a row. I know it like the back of my hand."

"But why is it only happening to you?" she asked. "Why isn't it happening to me or anyone else?"

"Believe me," I muttered. "I wish I knew."

11

DAY FOUR

Blindfolded, I felt my way into the kitchen.

"What are you doing?" I heard Jessica ask.

"You're wearing a black top and your short black skirt," I said. "You just got the top at the mall last night. In a second you're going to ask if I'm ready for the first day of school and you're going to tell me how immature I am because I plan to wedgy sixth-graders. You're eating granola and in a little while you'll get a ride to school with Cathy and her sister."

"So?"

I pulled off the blindfold. "Aren't you curious how I knew all that stuff?"

"It's easy, Jake," she said. "You probably saw what I was wearing before you put the blindfold on. And you knew what I was going to say because that's what I always say."

"Okay," I said. "How about this? Look out the window. There's a kid at the bus stop with blond hair and glasses. His name's Oliver but everyone calls him Ollie and he's new this year."

My sister looked out the window. "So?"

"So how did I know that?" I asked.

"I don't know, Jake," Jessica said, going back to the kitchen table. "And what's the point anyway?"

Somehow it wasn't working the way I'd hoped it would. Maybe it didn't matter. It had taken a lot of energy yesterday to convince my sister that I was living through the same day over and over again, and in the long run it didn't make a difference anyway.

I went over to the kitchen cabinet, got out the peanut butter and jelly, and started to make myself a sandwich.

"That's what you're having for breakfast?" Jessica wrinkled her nose.

"This is lunch."

"But Mom left you lunch money."

"Forget it," I said. "They're serving rancid cheeseburgers at school today."

Jessica looked at me like I'd lost my mind. "How do you know *that*?"

"Believe me," I said. "By the way, in about two minutes the town fire siren's gonna go off, then Cathy's sister is gonna pull up outside. A minute or two after that some fire engines are gonna pass here on their way to a house a couple of blocks over. Some new people just moved in and they left the toaster oven on this morning and the house is gonna be pretty much destroyed."

"Did anyone ever tell you you were certifiably insane?" Jessica asked.

I knew I wasn't. But if I didn't get out of the first day of school soon, I probably would be.

Everything happened exactly as it had the morning before. In homeroom I took my old seat, the one next to the empty seat where Amber Sweeny would soon sit.

Amber came in and sat down. Everyone gave her that starstruck look and I felt Alex nudge me.

"Talk to her," he whispered.

"Okay." I turned to Amber and said, "Hi."

"Hi." Amber smiled shyly.

"You must be new this year," I said.

Amber nodded and hooked her long brown hair back behind her ear, revealing a small gold hoop earring. She had to be about the most beautiful girl who'd ever set foot in Burp It Up Middle School.

"Where're you from?" I asked.

Out of the corner of my eye, I could see Alex staring at me in absolute astonishment. But as far as I was concerned, it was a no-lose situation. Even if I made a total fool of myself, all I had to do was wait until tomorrow.

"Boulder, Colorado," Amber said.

"No kidding!" I acted really surprised. "That's about my favorite place in the whole world!"

"Really?" Amber looked surprised, too.

"Oh, man, it's got the mountains and the best skiing," I said.

"Jake, what's going on back there?" Ms. Rogers asked.

I quickly turned around and faced the front. "Uh, nothing, Ms. Rogers."

Ms. Rogers went back to reading announcements. Out of the corner of my eye I glanced at Alex and got an amazed look. Then I glanced at Amber, who gave me a smile and a shrug to let me know she was sorry I'd gotten in trouble for talking to her.

The bell rang. Amber and I both got up.

"So what's your next class?" I asked as we walked out the door.

"Uh . . ." Amber looked down at her schedule. "English. Room one-oh-two."

"It's that way," I said, pointing up the hall. "The third door on your right."

"Thanks, uh . . ."

"Jake," I said, holding out my hand. "Jake Sherman."

Amber shook it. "Thanks, Jake. I'm Amber Sweeny."

"I know."

Amber frowned. "How?"

"Ms. Rogers read your name, remember?"

"Oh, yeah." Amber grinned self-consciously. "First day in a new school, you know? It's a little confusing."

"Sure," I said. "Gets you every time."

"Well, uh . . ." Amber smiled shyly again. "See you later."

"Right." I gave her a little wave and she headed up the hall. I turned to go in the opposite direction . . . and found Alex waiting for me.

"Colorado?" He squinted at me. "Have you ever been there?"

"Well, no," I admitted.

"Then how do you know it's such a great place?"

"I saw a show on TV."

"And what is this stuff about skiing?" he asked. "You don't ski."

"Well, I plan to someday," I said.

We started walking to our next class. "I can't believe you," Alex said in awe. "I mean, you were totally cool."

"Piece of cake," I said as if it were nothing.

Alex kept shaking his head in wonder. "I just never knew you were so suave with the ladies."

The funny thing was, neither did I.

12

Everything proceeded normally until lunch. Since I'd brought mine from home, I didn't get on line with Alex. Instead I waited until Amber came out of the lunch line with her salad, then I sort of "ran into her" at the cashier.

"Hey, how's it going?" I asked, acting like I was surprised to see her.

"Pretty good," Amber said with a warm smile. "It's just hard to get used to a new school."

"I bet," I said.

"How long have you been here?" she asked.

"It's starting to seem like forever," I said, then quickly added, "but actually since sixth grade."

Amber was looking around at the tables. I could tell she wanted to sit down and eat.

"Hey, I'm sorry," I said. "You must be hungry. I shouldn't be holding you up."

"Oh, no, it's okay," Amber replied quickly. "But maybe we should sit."

Since she said "we," I figured that meant me,

too. So we found an empty table and sat down together. I asked Amber why she'd moved from Boulder, and she said her mother had gotten a job here with a printing company. Her father was a management consultant and could work just about any place he liked.

"I guess the move wasn't so hard for my parents," Amber confided. "But I just feel like I've lost all my friends."

I glanced across the cafeteria to where Josh and Andy were sitting. "I know what you mean."

Amber frowned. "But I thought you've always lived here."

"Sometimes you don't have to move to lose your friends," I said.

Just then Ms. Rogers stopped by. "Well, Jake, I see you've made friends with Amber," she said.

I sort of shrugged like it was no big deal.

"Well, I think it's nice," Ms. Rogers said. "Jake's a nice boy, Amber. I wish I could say the same for some of his friends."

Alex was coming toward us with a lunch tray. Ms. Rogers moved to the next table.

"Hi, Jake," Alex said with a funny grin. "Can I join you guys?"

"Sure," I said. He sat down and I introduced him to Amber.

"So, I see you've met Jake," Alex said.

Amber nodded and smiled.

"Yeah, old Jake." Alex gave me a playful nudge

on the shoulder. "We call him the ladies' man. Every time a new girl comes to school, he always gets to know her first."

"Really?" Amber gave me a curious look.

"No way," I said. "That's totally bogus. Nobody calls me the ladies' man."

"Oh, come on, Jake," Alex said. "Fess up."

I didn't know whether Alex made up the story to make me look bad or good. But either way, I didn't appreciate him saying that stuff in front of Amber. Not knowing what to say, I opened my lunch bag and took out my peanut butter and jelly sandwich.

"Hey, what's with the brown bag, dude?" Alex asked as he picked up his cheeseburger. "Your folks can't afford to give you lunch money?"

Alex was being completely obnoxious, probably to show off in front of Amber. I had planned to tell him the real reason I'd brought lunch from home, but now I changed my mind. Alex took a big bite of his cheeseburger and started to chew.

"We call Alex Mr. Manners," I told Amber, "because he's got such good table manners."

Suddenly Alex stopped chewing. His face turned kind of white and his eyes darted around.

"Something wrong, Mr. Manners?" I asked innocently.

"*Mmmfff.*" Alex made a funny sound. Now his face started to turn red.

"Some people talk with food in their mouths,"

I said to Amber. "But not Mr. Manners. He's much too refined."

"*Blech!*" The words were hardly out of *my* mouth when the half-chewed cheeseburger came flying out of *his*. It landed in a glob on the table. Alex quickly took a loud slurp of orange drink, rinsed out his mouth, and spit it out on the floor.

Amber's jaw fell and her green eyes widened.

"Why, Mr. Manners," I said to Alex, trying not to smile. "That's so unlike you."

Alex excused himself and disappeared for the rest of lunch. Later Amber and I walked over to Mr. Dirksen's class. Once again, Mr. Dirksen sprang the test on us, and once again I got him to agree that anyone who aced it wouldn't have to take his class for the rest of the year.

I took the test and thought I did pretty well. There were still a couple of questions I wasn't quite certain of, but I figured if I didn't ace it today, there'd always be tomorrow.

After class Alex and I stopped by our lockers to dump some books.

"So how're things with Amber?" he asked glumly.

"Okay."

"What'd she say at lunch?" he asked.

"Just how she's gonna miss the mountains and her friends and stuff."

"What else?" Alex asked.

"Not much. I said I'd show her around town after school today."

"You mean, like a date?" Alex gasped in wonder as we started down the hall.

"Well, not really."

But Alex seemed mighty impressed. "You're unreal, dude! At this rate, you'll probably get her out to the cliff by tomorrow."

The cliff was in Jeffersonville Park. It wasn't much of a cliff, really, but it had a view of Jefferson Lake, and it was the place where couples went to make out.

"No way," I said.

"But just think if you did, dude," Alex said. "You'd be a living legend at Burp It Up. The guy who got Amber Sweeny up to the cliff on the second day of school."

The idea of being a legend sort of appealed to me, although I wasn't sure getting Amber to go to the cliff was the way I wanted to do it.

"Hey, look who's coming," Alex said.

I didn't have to look. I knew it was Ollie.

Once again, Alex started to drag him toward the girls' room. As usual, I was supposed to watch for teachers.

Today I didn't see any teachers. Alex shoved Ollie into the girls' room and held the door while Ollie banged on it and shouted to let him out. The usual bunch of kids stopped to see what was going on. Then we heard Amber's voice join Ollie's, and Alex let go of the door.

That's when I just happened to step into a doorway where Amber couldn't see me. The girls' room door swung open and Ollie hurried out and started down the hall. Alex looked at the crowd around him and smiled proudly. Then Amber came out and glared at him.

"Grow up," she said, and walked away.

The crowd laughed and Alex turned a deep shade of red.

Just before the end of school I stopped at my locker to drop off some books. Alex was waiting for me, and he didn't look happy.

"Where were you?" he asked.

"When?" I played dumb.

"When Amber Sweeny came out of the girls' room and made me look like an idiot in front of half the school."

"Oh, uh, I had to go sharpen a pencil," I said.

"What?" Alex scowled at me, but before he could say anything else, Mr. Dirksen came up.

"Jake, I'm amazed," he said.

"Uh?" I pretended I didn't know what he was talking about, either.

"You almost got a perfect score," Mr. Dirksen said. "In fact, if you hadn't gotten the pseudopod mixed up with the flagellum, you would have."

"And then I could have skipped your class all year and still gotten a *A*?" I asked.

"That's right." Mr. Dirksen nodded.

"Well, maybe next time," I said.

Mr. Dirksen frowned. "But there won't be a next time."

That's what you think, I thought.

"Well, I've got to go," Mr. Dirksen said. "See you tomorrow."

He left and Alex looked at me with astonished eyes. "You are *amazing!*" he cried. "Do you realize you almost had a chance to become a legend *twice* today?"

All I could do was smile.

Just wait.

After school I showed Amber around town. Since neither of us had had much for lunch, we were hungry. We stopped at My Hero to share a cold Italian sub. She took a bite and her beautiful eyes lit up.

"This is much better than anything we have in Boulder," she said.

"There you go," I said. "Jeffersonville isn't all that bad."

"Guess not," she said with a smile.

After that we wandered into Disk Master and looked at the rows of CDs.

Suddenly Amber stopped. "Hear that?"

I paused and listened to the store music. Some

guy was singing about Norwegian Wood. "Yeah?"

"It's the Beatles," Amber said. "I used to have a baby-sitter who listened to them all the time. I think they're neat."

"My sister has some tapes of theirs," I said. At that moment I happened to glance out the window, and saw a familiar face spying on us. It was Alex. I waved at him to get lost.

"Who was that?" Amber asked. I guess she'd only caught a glimpse of him.

"Uh, no one," I said. "Guess we better get going, huh?"

"Okay."

We went outside and started to walk home. It turned out that Amber and her folks had just moved into 43 Walnut Street.

"That's only a couple of blocks away," I said. "How come I didn't see you at the bus stop this morning?"

"My dad drove me," Amber said. "We left pretty early, but of course we got totally lost. That's why I was late for homeroom."

We got to my corner and stopped.

"I could walk you home," I offered.

"No, it's all right," Amber said. "I'm pretty sure I can find my way from here."

"Well, okay." I scuffed my foot on the sidewalk, not knowing what to say next.

"It was really nice of you to show me around," Amber said, flashing her beautiful smile.

"Hey, no problem," I said.

"And thanks for everything today," she said. "I was really dreading it, you know? But you made it a lot nicer than it might have been."

"Anytime," I said.

"See ya tomorrow." Amber waved and started away. I waved back. I'd always thought beautiful girls were stuck up and snotty, but Amber was just plain nice.

Jessica was sitting in the living room when I got home.

"Where have you been?" she asked.

"I showed this new girl around town," I said.

"You sure?" she asked suspiciously.

"Yeah, why?"

"How did you know about that fire this morning?"

"I . . ." Hadn't I explained it all that morning?

"Cathy's cousin Charlie said they served bad cheeseburgers at lunch today," Jessica said. "How did you know about that?"

Now that I thought of it, maybe I hadn't explained it this morning. I stepped into the living room, planning to sit down and explain everything. But Jessica quickly jumped up and stood behind the chair.

"Not too close, Jake," she warned.

"What?"

"I don't know what's going on, but I don't like it," Jessica said.

"And I don't know what you're talking about."

"I'm talking about what you did today," Jessica said accusingly. "I heard you planning things with that jerk Alex on the phone last night. I now you planned to wedgy all the sixth-graders. The part I didn't hear was that you were going to burn down a house and try to poison the whole school."

"You've gone psycho," I said.

"Then how could you know about those things before they happened?" Jessica asked.

"Because this is the fourth day in a row that I've gone to the first day of school," I tried to explain. "I know everything that's going to happen."

Jessica backed away from the chair toward the stairs. "You expect me to believe that?"

"You have to believe it," I said. "It's true."

Jessica reached the banister. "Of course, Jake. I believe you." The next thing I knew, she ran up the stairs.

"Hey! Where are you going!" I yelled.

"Don't try to stop me!" Jessica yelled back.

I ran to the bottom of the stairs. *Bang!* A door slammed upstairs.

"What are you doing?" I shouted. I ran up the stairs and tried her door, but it was locked.

"It's for your own good!" Jessica shouted from inside.

"What are you talking about?" I yelled.

Inside, I could hear Jessica on the phone. "Hello, Mom? I think you better come home right away. No, no, everybody's okay, but we have a problem with Jake. A *big* problem."

Of course, the joke was on Jessica, even though it wasn't one I wanted to play. She got both of my parents to come home from work early, but when they called the fire department, the fire chief insisted that the blaze wasn't arson. They had traced it to the toaster oven. The same thing happened when my father called the board of education. The district nutritionist said the meat problem had been caused by a faulty refrigeration unit in the Burp-It-Up kitchen.

My parents were really mad at Jessica, but I finally got some time to brush up on my pseudopods and flagellums. I couldn't wait until the next day.

13

DAY FIVE

The next morning I was in a really great mood.

"What's with you?" Jessica asked, watching me from the kitchen table where she was eating her granola.

"Huh?" I looked up from the toast I was buttering.

"You're whistling."

"Oh, uh, yeah." I couldn't help smiling.

"You didn't forget that it's the first day of school, did you?"

"Nope." I munched on a piece of toast.

"Of course not, Mr. Big Shot. This is the day you and Alex conquer the world, right?"

I wasn't going to argue with her. Instead, I said, "Hey, do you still have that old Beatles tape?"

"Uh, I think so."

"Think I could borrow it?" I opened a cabinet

and took out the small plastic cooler my parents used on trips.

"I guess so." Jessica scowled. "What are you doing with the cooler?"

"Just taking it to school." I opened the refrigerator and took out the freeze packs we used to keep things cold.

"Aren't you going to put anything else in there?" Jessica asked after I put the freeze packs in the cooler.

"Not yet," I said. "By the way, you think I could catch a ride with you to school this morning?"

"How did you know I was getting a ride?" Jessica asked.

"Just a guess."

"Well, I guess it'll be okay."

"And do you think we could stop at My Hero on the way?" I asked.

"Why?" Jessica looked at me like I'd flipped.

"I just want to pick up something for lunch," I said.

I got Cathy's sister to stop at the sub shop just long enough for me to run inside and buy a cold Italian hero. At school I met Alex at our lockers.

"Hey, I thought we were gonna meet at the bus stop this morning," he said, holding the letter with his combination.

"Something came up," I said. "So how'd it go?"

Before he could answer, Ollie ran up to us red-faced and out of breath, so I knew Alex had made him run around the block.

"Why, if it isn't Ollie from Ohio," Alex said, then turned to me. "Ollie's a new sixth-grader and it looks like he missed the bus."

"You made me miss it," Ollie gasped.

"Now, now, Ollie, you just have to learn to run faster," Alex said.

"Anyway, now I'm late and I can't find my homeroom," he said.

"And what room might that be, Ollie boy?" Alex asked.

"One-oh-six."

Alex gave him that awestruck look. "Oh, wow, that's all the way around to the other side of school!" he gasped, giving me a wink.

"Don't listen to this goofball," I said. "It's just two doors down on your left."

"Okay, thanks." Ollie quickly jogged away.

"What'd you do that for?" Alex asked.

"You already made him run all the way to school," I said. "Don't you think that's enough?"

Alex shrugged and we went into homeroom. Amber showed up late as usual and Alex dared me to talk to her. Once again I did. Later in the hall Alex grilled me about Colorado and skiing.

"Dude, I can't believe you," he said in awe. "I mean, you were totally cool."

"Piece of cake," I said like it was nothing.

Alex kept shaking his head in wonder. "I never knew you were so suave with the ladies."

"Oh, yeah, always," I said with a smile. "Matter of fact, I bet I can get her to the cliff by this afternoon."

Alex laughed. "No way!"

"Bet?" I said.

"You'll lose big time."

"Put your money where your mouth is, dude."

"Okay, ten bucks says you can't do it," Alex said.

"Deal." We shook hands.

I didn't see Amber until lunch, when I once again "bumped" into her outside the cashier. We talked a little and then decided to sit down. Only this time, instead of bringing a peanut butter and jelly sandwich from home, I took the cold Italian hero out of the cooler.

"My favorite!" she gasped.

"Here, have half," I said, offering part to her.

"I couldn't," Amber said. "It's your lunch."

"It's cool, really," I said. "I can't eat the whole thing."

Amber accepted half of the sandwich, and we talked and laughed all through lunch. Ms. Rogers came by and said hi, but Alex stayed away because that was part of our deal.

After lunch, Amber and I walked to Mr. Dirksen's room and sat down together. A moment later Andy and Josh came in.

"Be right back," I told Amber.

I got up and went over to my old friends. I'd only planned to say hello, since I hadn't had a chance to talk to them at lunch.

"Look who's here," Josh said.

"Hey, guys, didn't see much of you this summer," I said, trying to be friendly.

"We were around," Andy said. "Where were you?"

"He was around," Josh answered before I could. "He just had cooler friends to hang out with."

"That's not exactly true," I said in a low voice so Alex wouldn't hear.

"Oh, yeah?" Josh asked. "Then how come we didn't see you all summer?"

"I don't know," I said defensively. "I guess it just went by really fast."

"We hear you're a really fast kind of guy these days," Andy said sarcastically. "Alex is telling everyone you bet him ten bucks you could get that new girl Amber Sweeny over to the cliff this afternoon."

That made me mad. Alex wasn't supposed to tell anyone.

"So cool," Josh muttered.

"It's a joke," I whispered. "I can't lose."

"Jake really thinks he's hot stuff," Andy said.

"Yeah," Josh said bitterly. "No wonder he doesn't want to hang out with dorks like us."

It wasn't fair. Here I was, trying to be friendly, and they wouldn't give me a chance. Then I got an idea.

"Hey," I said in a low voice. "I hear Dirksen's gonna give us a surprise test today."

"On the first day of school?" Andy shook his head. "No way."

"It's not gonna count," I said. "He just wants to see what we know."

It didn't take long to make another bet, this one for ten bucks each that I could ace the test. Of course, they had to promise to pay me by dinnertime.

A few minutes later I took the test for the fifth time. After class, Alex and I stopped by our lockers to dump our books.

"So how's it going, lover boy?" Alex asked.

"You weren't supposed to tell anyone about the bet," I said. "What if someone tells Amber?"

"Hey, don't worry," Alex said. "Everyone's cool."

We started down the hall and ran into Ollie. Once again, Alex shoved him into the girls' room and held the door while Ollie banged on it and shouted to let him out. The usual crowd of kids stopped to see what was going on.

"Let him out," I said.

"What?" Alex looked surprised.

"I said, let him out."

"Why?" Alex asked.

"Yeah, Jake," said a kid in the crowd. "It's funny."

"How would you like to be trapped in the girls' room?" I asked.

"Chill out, Jake," Alex said.

"You let him out or else," I said, making a fist. "I mean it, Alex."

Alex let go of the door and Ollie raced out and down the hall. Then Amber came out and fixed a steely gaze on Alex, who shrank back into the crowd.

"Grow up," she said with a glower. Then she turned to me and smiled. "I heard what you said."

"It's just not right to pick on little kids," I said. "Especially when they're new in town."

As we started to walk to our next class, I glanced back over my shoulder at Alex. He was staring at me with a totally dumbfounded look on his face.

Just before the end of school, I stopped at my locker to drop off some books. I knew Alex would be waiting for me, but I didn't expect to find Josh and Andy, too. And they didn't look happy.

"Hey, guys," I said a little warily.

"Nice going, Jake," Josh muttered.

"How'd you ace that test?" Andy asked.

I shrugged. "Luck, I guess."

"Bull," Josh said, reaching into his pocket and handing me ten dollars.

"Yeah, I don't know how you did it, Jake," Andy said, giving me his ten dollars, "but you really conned us."

"Way to go, *friend*," Josh said sourly. Then he turned to Andy. "Come on, let's get out of here before Jake figures out another way to rob us."

Josh and Andy left. I watched them walk away down the hall. Suddenly I felt really bad.

"Why the long face, dude?" Alex asked, coming up.

I wasn't about to tell him. Actually, I was surprised he was talking to me. "How come you're not mad that I made you let Ollie out of the girls' room?" I asked.

"I don't know," Alex said. "Maybe it was dumb to push him in there in the first place."

I nodded, still watching Josh and Andy walk away.

"Aw, don't worry about those chumps," Alex said. "They're just a couple of losers. I know why you made that bet with them."

"You do?" I asked, surprised.

"Sure," Alex said with a grin. "You just wanted to make sure you were covered when you lost your bet with me."

"Yeah, right," I said, feeling glum and wishing I had my old friends back.

After school I showed Amber around town just as I had the day before. Only this time I brought along a little boom box and played Jessica's old Beatles tape.

"You like them?" Amber stopped on the sidewalk and stared at me with raised eyebrows.

"Oh, yeah, they're one of my favorite groups."

"Mine, too!" Amber gasped.

For a second, Amber and I just looked into each other's eyes.

"It's so strange," she said. "But I feel like I've met you before."

Suddenly I had to look away.

"Uh, know what?" I said. "There's one other place I want to show you — Jeffersonville Park."

It wasn't hard to get Amber into the park, and once we were there I told her I wanted to show her the cliff because it had a good view. We were walking up the path when I saw Alex and a bunch of guys from school coming toward us.

"Hey, dude!" Alex grinned and winked. "Headin' for the cliff, huh?" All the kids with him smiled knowingly.

"Yeah," I said. "I'm just showing Amber around."

"Well, have a good time, dude," Alex said, and winked again.

Alex and his buddies continued down the path, and Amber and I headed for the cliff.

"What was that about?" Amber asked.

"Huh?" I played dumb.

"It seemed like they were waiting for you."

"Naw, a lot of people hang out in this park after school," I lied.

I took Amber up to the cliff and showed her the view. Then we walked home and stopped at my corner again. I pretended to be surprised that we both lived in the same neighborhood.

"I could walk you home," I said, knowing she'd say no.

"No, it's all right," Amber said. "I'm pretty sure I can find my way from here."

"Well, okay." I scuffed my foot on the sidewalk.

"It was really nice of you to show me around," Amber said, flashing her beautiful smile.

"No problem."

"And thanks for everything today," she said. "I was really dreading it, you know? But you made it a lot better than it could have been."

"Hey, anytime," I said, trying to smile.

"See ya tomorrow." Amber waved and started away. I waved back. For the second time that day I felt lousy about winning a bet. I'd used my friends, and then I'd used Amber.

Alex was waiting at my house. With a big smile he reached into his pocket and dug out a crumpled ten-dollar bill.

"Here you go, dude!" he said, giving it to me.

86

"I never saw anyone so happy about losing a bet," I said, putting the money in my wallet.

"Are you kidding?" Alex slapped me on the back. "It was worth it! Tomorrow everyone will know that my best bud is the dude who got Amber Sweeny up to the cliff on the first day of school! You're a legend, dude!"

I tried to smile, but somehow I didn't feel like a legend.

That night Jessica cooked vegetarian spaghetti again. Just the smell of it made me want to barf.

"So how was school, Mr. Big Shot?" she asked.

"Okay," I said. "Have you ever heard of someone having to go through the same day over and over?"

She gave me a strange look. "No, why?"

"Just wondering."

"So, did you wedgy everyone in sight?"

I shook my head. It was hard to believe that five days ago I thought that was the coolest thing in the world.

"What happened to all your plans with Alex?" she asked.

"I don't know."

"Is something wrong?" Jessica asked.

"You think tomorrow night we could have something other than spaghetti?"

"Of course. I never make the same dinner twice."

That's what you think, I thought.

Jessica gave me a funny look. "What's with you?"

"Nothing."

"Remember that fire this morning?" she asked.

"Yeah . . . er . . . I mean no . . . er, I mean yeah?" It was getting hard to keep track of what I was supposed to know and not know.

"It was just a few blocks over," she said. "A new family just moved in. I heard they left the toaster oven on. There's hardly anything left."

"That's really too bad," I said.

I spent the rest of the night watching TV. We had cable and got about sixteen channels so I figured I had sixteen days before I'd have to start renting videos. But it wasn't a very reassuring thought. How long could I go through the first day of school before I went crazy?

14

DAY SIX

Beep . . . beep . . . beep! The alarm went off but I didn't get out of bed. What was the point? I knew exactly what was going to happen. Why should I listen to Jessica give me a hard time again? Why bother hanging around with Alex and getting hassled by Josh and Andy? About the only thing I could look forward to was seeing Amber, but I really didn't want to play any more tricks on her. In fact, I wished I could go over to her house and just tell her the truth about the day before.

But it was a new first day of school and right now she didn't even know who I was.

Still, I wished I could go over to Walnut Street and see her.

Walnut Street . . .

WALNUT STREET!!!

I sat straight up in bed. The fire in the toaster oven. . . . The house was a couple of blocks over. . . . A new family . . .

Why hadn't I put it together sooner?

I jumped out of bed and quickly pulled on my clothes. They were the same clothes I'd worn the day before, but today they were clean again, so it didn't matter. Still tucking my shirt in, I stumbled out into the hall. Jessica, wearing an oversized T-shirt, was just coming out of her room.

"What are you doing?" she asked with a yawn.

"I've got to go somewhere."

"Now? What about the first day of school?"

"Don't worry."

"You're not going to skip it, are you?" she asked.

"Believe me, it doesn't matter."

I ran down the stairs and out the door. Walnut was three streets over. I had to hurry. Amber had said she and her father left early.

I ran down Bay Drive, past Cedar and Oak to Walnut. As I turned the corner, I saw a yellow car backing out of a driveway about halfway down the block. I started to run even faster. Luckily, the car turned toward me. It had green license plates. As I got closer I saw that they said COLORADO in white letters. I ran into the middle of the street, waving my arms for the car to stop.

The car stopped and Amber's father rolled down

his window. Like Amber, he had brown hair.

"Can I help you?" He looked puzzled. I could see Amber looking across the front seat at me.

"Listen," I said, gasping for breath. "You have to go back to your house. You left your toaster oven on."

"What? That can't be."

"Look, Mr. Sweeny," I gasped. "You have to believe me. Your house is gonna burn down."

Mr. Sweeny frowned. "Who are you? How do you know my name?"

"I don't have time to explain," I said. "Now, do you want to save your house or not?"

Mr. Sweeny looked across the seat at Amber and then back at me. "I'm sorry, son, but it's just not possible."

"It is," I insisted. "You have to believe me."

"But we don't own a toaster oven."

Huh? For a second I didn't understand. Then I thought maybe I did.

"Sure you do," I said. "Look, I can't argue with you now. Maybe they call it something else in Colorado, but if you don't get back in your house and turn it off, you're gonna have a fire."

Mr. Sweeny looked at Amber again and then back at me. "I think you have the wrong people, son." He started to close his window.

"Wait!" I shouted, putting my hand on the window. "You have to believe me. There's gonna be a fire. Your house is gonna burn down."

91

Whaaaaa-O-Whaaaaa-O-Whaaaa! The town's fire siren began to blast.

"You see?" I said.

Mr. Sweeny and Amber turned to look back at the house. Nothing unusual was happening. There was no smoke, no fire. . . . Mr. Sweeny looked at me.

"How did you know there was going to be a fire?" he asked.

"I don't get it," I said.

"Maybe it's just a coincidence, right, son?" Mr. Sweeny said.

Eeeeiiiiirrrrnnnn! Eeeeiiiiirrrrnnnn! Now we could hear the sounds of the fire trucks in the distance. The sirens gradually grew louder as the trucks came nearer. Once again we all looked back at the Sweenys' house. There was still nothing unusual.

Then I noticed a plume of black smoke rising in the air. It was coming from one street over: Maple!

"It's not your house!" I gasped.

A second later the big red-and-silver pumper truck raced past on Bay Drive with its lights flashing, followed by the second truck. I started running toward Maple Street. When I got there, the firemen were already pulling hoses off the pumper and hooking them up to the fire hydrant. The second house in from the corner was burning. Flames leaped out of some of the windows, along with thick black smoke.

A crowd of neighbors was forming on the sidewalk to watch as the firemen began to spray powerful streams of water into the windows and on the roof.

"Who lives there?" I heard a woman with her hair in rollers ask.

"I don't know," said another woman wearing a pink robe and fuzzy slippers. "I think they just moved in yesterday."

"Was anyone home?"

"I don't think so."

"Oh, those poor people."

I watched them fight the fire. Imagine living in a house for just one day and then coming home and finding it destroyed.

Then I realized I had to get to school. Of course, I didn't really have to go through the first day again, but if I didn't, it would be super hard to explain to my parents and the school why not.

I got down to the bus stop just in time to see Alex order everyone to stand in a row. When he saw me, he raised his hand high. "Sir Jake, dude!"

"Hi, Alex." I gave him a high five.

"Are we the Knights of Wedgy?" Alex asked loudly enough for everyone to hear.

"Uh, listen, can I talk to you for a second?" I said, motioning him away from the group.

"Sure, what's up?" Alex asked.

"I know last night I agreed to be a Knight of Wedgy," I said in a low voice. "But I changed my mind. Let's just go to school, okay? No wedgies."

Alex stared at me. "Chicken?"

I stared back at him. Now I understood why Amber told him to grow up. "Yeah." I nodded. "I'm a big fat chicken."

"Then I'll do it myself," Alex said, turning back to the group. The only kid who wasn't in line was Ollie.

Alex peered down at him and rubbed his chin. "Hmmm. What manner of creature is this? Must be a dweeb. Tell me, dweeb, do you have trouble hearing?"

Ollie shook his head.

"Leave him alone," I said.

Alex turned and frowned at me. "What's with you?"

"I told you, I don't want to pick on anyone."

Alex stared past me across the street, where old Mr. MacDowell was just coming out of his house.

"Okay, then watch this," he said, going across the street, and moving the garbage can into the driveway. But before Mr. MacDowell could hit it, I went over and moved it out of the way.

"What'd you do that for?" Alex asked when I came back to the bus stop.

"Just give it a rest," I said.

The bus came and we all got on. Alex went to the back. "Okay, everyone, move out. Eighth-graders only."

The other kids moved and Alex waved to me. "Come on, dude. We've got the back of the bus. Eighth-grade privileges."

Ollie had taken a seat near the front. He was looking up at me.

"I'm gonna sit here," I told Alex and sat down next to the sixth-grader. "Hi, bet your name's Ollie."

He gave me an astonished look. "How'd you know?"

All I could do was smile. "It's a long story."

We got to school and I helped Ollie with his locker combination and showed him where his homeroom was. When I got to my homeroom, Alex waved to me from the back, but I took a seat across the room instead. When Amber came in I hid my face in a book so she wouldn't notice me.

At lunch I sat with Andy and Josh and warned them about the cheeseburgers. Then I told them about the surprise science test and what the answers would be. I'd taken the test so many times that I knew it by heart. Josh and Andy both made up little crib sheets.

In Mr. Dirksen's class I took a seat in the front

with Andy and Josh, and hid my face again so Amber wouldn't see me when she came in. I got Mr. Dirksen to agree let anyone who aced the test skip this class for the rest of the year. Andy and Josh used their crib sheets. After class we met in the hall.

"How'd you guys do?" I asked.

"I'm sure I aced it!" Josh said. "You gave us every single answer!"

"Yeah." Andy grinned. "I wish we could be there when Dirksen marks it. He's gonna freak!"

"Guess we're all gonna have a free period after lunch for the rest of the year!" Josh slapped me on the back. "Way to go, Jake!"

The three of us gave each other high fives and laughed. It was just like old times.

Suddenly we noticed a commotion down the hall. Alex was pushing Ollie into the girls' room and the usual crowd was gathering around them.

"Silver's such a jerk," Andy muttered.

"Hey, cool it," cautioned Josh. "He's Jake's good buddy now."

"Forget it," I said, "the guy's a bozo."

Once again I went down the hall and told Alex to let Ollie out of the girls' room or else. Alex let go of the door and Ollie hurried out, followed by Amber. Our eyes locked for a second, but before she could say anything I turned and took off.

*   *   *

At the end of the day I went to my locker to put away some books before I caught the bus home.

"Jake?"

I turned around and found Mr. Dirksen with Josh and Andy. Mr. Dirksen looked serious. Josh and Andy had sheepish looks on their faces.

"I find it very interesting that you three close friends somehow managed to get perfect scores on the test this afternoon," he said. "Could you please explain that to me?"

"Sure," I said with a grin. "We're all brilliant."

Mr. Dirksen wasn't amused. "I don't know how you found out about it, but I'm certain you did. And now I assume that all three of you expect to skip my class the rest of the year."

"Well, that's the deal we made," I said.

"You're right," Mr. Dirksen said. "And a deal's a deal. So all I'll need is a letter from each of your parents stating that they agree that you don't have to take science this year."

"But that's not fair," Josh complained.

"I'm sorry, Josh, but I can't excuse students from my class for the entire year without their parents' consent," Mr. Dirksen said. "And don't bother forging the letters because I'll be calling each of your homes to confirm."

Mr. Dirksen left. Josh, Andy, and I looked at each other and shrugged.

"Come on," Josh said. "We better get out to

the parking lot or we'll miss our buses."

We started walking.

"You gonna ask your parents for a letter?" Andy asked.

Josh shook his head. "Get real. They'll never let me skip class for the whole year."

"Neither will mine," I said.

Andy nodded. "Mine, neither. Well, I just wish we could've been there when Dirksen graded those things. I bet he really wigged."

We all smiled at the thought.

"You guys didn't tell him I gave you the answers, did you?" I asked.

"No way!" Josh looked offended. "What do you think we are?"

I smiled. Josh and Andy would never squeal. On the other hand, I had a feeling Alex probably would have spilled his guts in no time.

"So you doin' anything after school?" Andy asked me.

"Naw, what about you?"

"Want to play some ball?"

"Sure."

"Great," Josh said. "We'll meet at my house."

We got out to the parking lot and split up to catch our buses. It was good to have my old friends back.

The first person I saw on the bus home was Ollie, so I sat down next to him.

"How're you doin'?" I asked as the bus pulled away from school.

"Okay," he said. "Thanks for getting me out of the girls' room before."

"No sweat. How was the first day of school?"

"Okay, I guess," Ollie said.

"You're new in town, right?"

"I'll say. We just moved in yesterday."

"Yesterday?" For some reason that sounded vaguely familiar.

"Yeah," Ollie said. "It was a real last-minute thing. My father got a transfer and we had to move really quick so that I could start the year in a new school."

Something about this was beginning to bother me. "How come you got to the bus stop so early this morning?" I asked.

"Well, my parents had to go away for the day and I didn't want to stay home alone so I figured I'd wait at the bus stop," he said.

It was starting to bother me more. "What street do you live on?"

"Maple Street," Ollie said as the bus bumped and squeaked along. Why?"

"Which house?"

"Second one from the corner." Ollie gave me a puzzled look. I felt dizzy, like all the blood had drained out of my face.

"What'd you have for breakfast this morning?" I asked, praying I was mistaken.

"Some waffles."

Suddenly I felt relieved. "Made them in a waffle iron?"

"No, they were frozen," Ollie said. "I made them in the toaster oven."

15

We got off at the bus stop. I knew I couldn't let Ollie walk home alone and find that his home had burned down, so I pretended my house was near his.

"So, uh, will your parents be home when you get there?" I asked.

Ollie gave me another funny look and then shook his head. "They said they wouldn't be home until late. Why?"

"Just asking. Tell you what? Want to hang out at my house until they come home?"

Ollie frowned. "Thanks, but I better get home. They might try to call."

A sense of dread was growing inside me with every step. Ollie was just about to have the worst shock of his life, and there was nothing I could do to stop it.

As we turned the corner and started walking up Maple Street, a faint smell of smoke was in the air. I glanced at Ollie, but he didn't seem to notice it. Then Ollie's house came into view. Maybe I should say, what was left of Ollie's house. The walls and part of the roof were still standing, but the house was charred and gutted. Every window was broken and the lawn was covered with smoldering chairs and couches the firefighters had pulled out from inside.

Ollie stopped and blinked. Then he started to run toward the house.

"Ollie!" I started to run after him. "Ollie, don't go inside!"

He stopped halfway up the driveway and just looked around. Tears ran down his cheeks, and he took off his glasses and wiped his eyes with his hand. For a long time he didn't say anything. Then he turned and looked up at me.

"You knew about this," he said. "That's why you were so friendly to me. That's why you walked with me."

I shook my head. "I knew this house had burned, but I didn't know it was yours until we were on the bus just now."

"How'd it happen?"

"I heard it was . . ." I stopped myself.

"What?" Ollie asked.

"Nothing," I said. There was no point in telling him he'd left the toaster oven on. It would only make him feel worse. "Is there any way you can get in touch with your parents?"

Ollie shook his head. "They had to go to the city

on business. They told me to come home after school and wait for them."

We left a note saying that he'd be at my house. We walked over there and sat in the kitchen eating potato chips and drinking Cokes.

Then Jessica came home and I told her what had happened.

"That's terrible," Miss Politically Correct said. "What time do you think your parents will get home?"

"I don't know," he said. "They warned me it might be kind of late."

"Maybe you ought to stay for dinner," she said. "I'm making spaghetti."

"Couldn't you make something else?" I asked.

Jessica frowned. "What's wrong with my spaghetti?"

"I . . . er . . . Ollie may not be used to vegetarian spaghetti."

"It's okay," Ollie said. "I don't have much of an appetite anyway."

I sighed. It looked like I was going to be eating that disgusting spaghetti for the sixth night in a row.

We sat around and Ollie talked about moving here from Ohio, and how everything was so new. New house (until this morning), new neighborhood, new school, new grade.

"In fifth grade you're one of the big kids," he

said. "Then you get to middle school and suddenly you're a little kid all over again. And all these big kids want to push you around."

"The eighth-graders are the worst," Jessica said, shooting me a look from the kitchen counter.

"I'll say." Ollie nodded in agreement.

I shrank down in my seat and didn't say a word.

"I bet you'll want to push the sixth-graders around when you're in eighth grade," Jessica said, making sure I heard.

"I hope not," Ollie said.

"I think that's very mature of you," Jessica said, giving me another pointed look.

If I'd slouched down any farther in my chair I probably would have wound up on the floor.

We were in the middle of dinner when the doorbell rang. Ollie instantly looked up.

"I bet that's your folks," I said, getting up. "Better get your stuff."

I went to the front door and opened it. A short, grim-looking man wearing a suit and glasses was standing there. He had the same sandy-colored hair as Ollie. Standing behind him was a woman trying to rub tears out of her eyes.

"Are you Jake Sherman?" the man asked.

"Yes. Ollie's just getting his stuff," I said. "I'm really sorry about your house."

Ollie's father nodded and his mother sniffled. Ollie came up behind me and went through the doorway.

"Thank God, you're all right!" His mom cried and hugged him.

Ollie's father held out his hand. "Thank you, Jake. Thank you very much."

I watched as Ollie's parents led him back to their car. They'd come all the way from Ohio and now they had no place to live. They'd probably lost all their possessions, too.

Just before they got in the car, Ollie turned and waved. "See you tomorrow."

I waved back, and watched as they drove away. Suddenly it occurred to me that I should have invited them to stay at our house for the night. But by then it was too late. The car turned the corner and disappeared. I didn't know where they were going. I went back to the kitchen where Jessica was waiting for me.

"Were you one of the eighth-graders who picked on him?" she asked.

"No."

"What happened to all your plans with Alex? I thought you two were supposed to be the Knights of Wedgy today."

"I guess I changed my mind," I said with a shrug.

"Wow," Jessica said. "That means there still might be hope for you."

I tried to smile, but it wasn't easy. The truth was, things looked pretty hopeless.

16

DAY SEVEN

Beep . . . beep . . . beep! As soon as the alarm went off I jumped out of bed and got dressed. As I stepped out into the upstairs hall, Jessica opened her door. She rubbed her eyes and yawned.

"Where are you going?"

"I have to take care of something," I said.

"What about breakfast?"

"I'll get something at school." I dashed downstairs and out of the house. The dew was still on the grass, and grown-ups wearing suits were walking out of their houses and heading for the train station.

I ran down Bay Drive and turned onto Maple. A moment later I jogged up Ollie's driveway, and rang the doorbell.

"Uh, who is it?" Ollie asked from inside.

"Jake Sherman," I said. "I'm an eighth-grader and I've been assigned to help you through the first day of school because you're new here. I'm supposed to make sure you find the bus stop and get your locker open and find your homeroom."

But Ollie didn't open the door. "Nobody told us about that."

"That's probably because you just moved in yesterday," I ad-libbed.

"Well, okay," Ollie said. "But would you mind waiting outside? I'm here alone and my parents told me not to let anyone in."

"Uh, normally I would, Ollie, but I really need to use the bathroom."

"How'd you know to call me Ollie?" he asked through the door.

"Uh, I didn't," I quickly said. "It was just an accident. I, er, had a friend named Oliver once and we called him Ollie, too."

"Well, I'm sorry, but you'll have to wait," Ollie said. "I really promised my parents I wouldn't let anyone in."

I had no choice but to wait. After a while, Ollie came out and gave me a funny look. "You *sure* you're from school?"

"Positive," I said. "And the first thing I'm supposed to do is make sure you've turned off all your appliances."

"Huh?" Ollie looked at me very strangely.

"The school doesn't want any homes burning down."

"I'm sure it's okay," Ollie said.

"I'm sure, too," I said. "But you don't want me to get in trouble with the school, do you?"

"Well, okay, wait a second." Ollie went back inside. A moment later he came back out. "Okay, let's go."

"Uh, you *sure* you checked *all* your appliances?" I asked. It seemed like he'd been in and out awful fast.

"Yeah." Ollie started down the driveway, then stopped and looked back at me. "Now what?"

"Well, er, uh . . ." I had to think fast. "There was just a story on the news last night about faulty toaster ovens. You wouldn't happen to have a toaster oven, would you?"

Ollie nodded.

"Wow," I said. "Would you do me a super-huge favor and check it again? Just to make sure."

"Are you for real?" Ollie looked at me like I was a total dork.

"That's all I ask," I said. "Okay?"

Ollie rolled his eyes and went back into the house again. This time he stayed inside a little longer, and when he came out, he looked at me suspiciously.

"That was weird," he said. "The toaster oven

was still on. And it was really hot. I bet it could have started a fire."

Whew! A huge feeling of relief spread through me. That was close.

The rest of the day went pretty well. I protected Ollie from Alex, and sat next to Amber again. I talked to her, but this time I didn't make any bets with anyone. And while I was friendly to Andy and Josh, I didn't give them advance warning about Mr. Dirksen's test. I did warn them about the cheeseburgers, and at lunch the three of us sat with Amber.

It was tough not to put down all the right answers on the test, but I figured I'd save them for when it really counted. After school I showed Amber around town for a while and then went over to Josh's to play ball. I even invited Alex so that we could play two-on-two. He turned out to be a decent basketball player, and we all had a good time.

"So how was school, Mr. Big Shot?" Jessica asked that night in the kitchen as she started to boil the water for spaghetti.

"Hey," I said. "What do you say we order in a pizza?"

Jessica frowned. "Mom didn't leave us money."

"I'll pay," I said. I was so sick of her vegetarian spaghetti I would have paid *double* for a pizza.

"Did I hear you right?" Jessica asked. *"You're* going to pay for a pizza for *both* of us?"

"I'll even order half vegetarian," I said, knowing that was her favorite politically correct pizza.

Jessica stared at me suspiciously. "Is there something you're not telling me? Did you break something of mine? Or is there some huge favor you're going to ask?"

"No." I smiled. "I just want you to know how much I appreciate having a big sister."

Jessica got the portable phone and handed it to me. "Here. Order it fast before you change your mind."

17

DAY EIGHT

Beep . . . beep . . . beep! I opened my eyes. I couldn't believe I was going to do it all over again but what choice did I have? I jumped out of bed, pulled on my clothes, and headed out. As I stepped into the upstairs hall, Jessica opened her door. This time she just rubbed her eyes, yawned, and shook her head.

Outside, the dew was on the grass again and the grown-ups were heading for work. I arrived at Ollie's house about the same time I had the day before and rang the bell.

A moment later the door opened and I found myself facing Ollie's mom.

"Yes?" she looked a little puzzled.

"Uh, you're not supposed to be here," I said.

Ollie's mom scowled, then smiled as if she

111

understood. "We just moved in. You must be looking for the Kreegers, the people who used to live here."

"No, I'm looking for Ollie," I said.

Just then Ollie came up behind his mom. "Oh, hi, Jake, don't tell me you've been assigned to help me again."

Again?

Now his mom smiled. "You must be the nice boy Ollie told us about last night."

Last night? "Uh, I didn't know Ollie last night," I said.

Ollie and his mom gave each other strange looks. Then Ollie said, "Come on, Jake. Stop kidding. You came here yesterday to make sure I got to school okay. The toaster oven, remember?"

"You mean, today's not yesterday?" I asked.

Both Ollie and his mother frowned.

"What I meant was, today's not the first day of school?" I said.

"Of course not," Ollie's mom said. "Yesterday was the first day of school."

"I don't believe it!" I cried. "It's the second day of school!"

Ollie and his mom looked at me like I was nuts.

"I don't think we'll need your help today," his mom said, putting her arm protectively around Ollie's shoulder. "I think he'll be able to find the way himself."

"See you at school, Jake." Ollie waved, and his mother closed the door.

I staggered back down the driveway. *It was the second day of school!* I couldn't believe it! Out in the street I started to run home. As I crossed Walnut, a horn beeped and a yellow car with green Colorado license plates stopped in front of me. Amber rolled down her window.

"Need a ride to school, Jake?" she asked.

"Uh . . . uh, sure!"

Then Amber looked at my clothes and frowned. "Didn't you go home last night?"

"Well, yeah," I said. "What makes you think —" Suddenly I stopped and looked down at my clothes . . . *They were the same clothes I'd worn yesterday!*

"On second thought, thanks for the offer," I said. "But I think I'll just go home first and change."

"Okay, see you at school," Amber said.

When I got home, Jessica was sitting at the kitchen table, eating granola.

"How come you went out early again this morning?" she asked.

"Uh, I just had to," I said, heading for the stairs.

"And you won't tell me why, right?" she said.

"You wouldn't believe it anyway," I said as I started up the stairs.

"How many more mornings is this going to go on?" she called.

Halfway up the stairs I stopped. "You know what?" I yelled back happily. "I think it's finally over!"

About the Author

Todd Strasser has written many award-winning novels for young and teenage readers. Among his best-known books are *Help! I'm Trapped in Obedience School* and *Abe Lincoln for Class President!* His most recent project for Scholastic was *Camp Run-a-Muck*, a series about a summer camp where anything can happen.

Todd speaks frequently at schools about the craft of writing and conducts writing workshops for young people. He and his family live outside New York City with their yellow Labrador retriever, Mac.

You can find out more about Todd and his books at http://www.ToddStrasser.com

APPLE®PAPERBACKS

Pick an Apple and Polish Off Some Great Reading!

BEST-SELLING APPLE TITLES

- ☐ MT43944-8 **Afternoon of the Elves** Janet Taylor Lisle — **$3.99**
- ☐ MT41624-3 **The Captive** Joyce Hansen — **$3.50**
- ☐ MT43266-4 **Circle of Gold** Candy Dawson Boyd — **$3.99**
- ☐ MT44064-0 **Class President** Johanna Hurwitz — **$3.50**
- ☐ MT45436-6 **Cousins** Virginia Hamilton — **$3.99**
- ☐ MT43130-7 **The Forgotten Door** Alexander Key — **$3.99**
- ☐ MT44569-3 **Freedom Crossing** Margaret Goff Clark — **$3.99**
- ☐ MT42858-6 **The Hot and Cold Summer** Johanna Hurwitz — **$3.99**
- ☐ MT22514-2 **The House on Cherry Street 2: The Horror** Rodman Philbrick and Lynn Harnett — **$3.50**
- ☐ MT41708-8 **The Secret of NIMH** Robert C. O'Brien — **$4.50**
- ☐ MT42882-9 **Sixth Grade Sleepover** Eve Bunting — **$3.50**
- ☐ MT42537-4 **Snow Treasure** Marie McSwigan — **$3.99**

Available wherever you buy books, or use this order form

Scholastic Inc., P.O. Box 7502, 2931 East McCarty Street, Jefferson City, MO 65102

Please send me the books I have checked above. I am enclosing $_____ (please add $2.00 to cover shipping and handling). Send check or money order—no cash or C.O.D.s please.

Name_____**Birthdate**_____

Address_____

City_____**State/Zip**_____

Please allow four to six weeks for delivery. Offer good in U.S. only. Sorry, mail orders are not available to residents of Canada. Prices subject to change. 　　　　APP997